THE DESTRUCTION OF FAITH

Book 1

QUEEN ZOAYA COUNTS

Copyright © 2021 by Queen Zoaya Counts

All rights reserved. Published by Zoaya Works LLC.

No part of this book may be reproduced in any form or by any electronic or mechanical means, including information storage and retrieval systems, without written permission from the author, except for the use of brief quotations in a book review.

This is a work of fiction. Names, characters, places, and incidents either are the products of the author's imagination or are used fictitiously. Any resemblance to actual persons, living or dead, events, or locales is entirely coincidental.

Edited by Theresa Raines
Cover design by debb_design@fiverr.com
Formatted by Tapioca Press

ISBN 978-0-578-25591-0

Content Warnings: sexual content, violence, drug use

For those who fear the unknown

CHAPTER 1
SUNDAY MORNING

I AWAKE to the sounds of gospel music blaring from the radio in the kitchen. This Sunday morning ritual had been going on with my Mama for years.

Since I was twelve years old, I have had to endure her practice, playing gospel music every Sunday morning. She had to give Sunday to the Lord because she gave them to the devil during the other days of the week.

Even now that I am twenty-one, I still must engage in this ritual by getting up out of bed, washing my face, brushing my teeth, and then to the kitchen to eat breakfast. Mama would have my plate already prepared to eat; three pancakes, two slices of bacon, and scrambled eggs with cheese. She would stand there in her black dress, with her off-black stockings trying to slip down on her legs, wearing her house slippers, smoking on a Salem cigarette, and leaning against the kitchen sink. She would stand there watching me eat my breakfast.

Once I finished eating, she would take my plate and hand me a blue dress to put on, and tell me to hurry up and get my shoes so I would not be late for Sunday school. We then would walk outside the house and wait on the blue bus to pick us up. I hated that damn bus.

I grabbed the pillow and covered my face, trying to force the sounds of the gospel music from my head.

"Push harder," I hear a voice whisper to me. I push the pillow harder into my face as if I am smothering myself. I can feel my air leaving me; then, suddenly, it's snatched off my face.

"Why are you still in bed?" I hear. I opened my eyes to focus as I saw my Mama standing there glaring down at me. I look at her, and she is wearing that black dress that still looks brand new.

"Ma, no. I am not going to church," I wanted to scream at her, but I just mumbled it.

"What you mean you are not going? Sunday is the Lord's day, and you are going with me to church," she shouted.

"I said I'm not going," I repeated. I sniff the air as I smell cigarette smoke. "Mom, can you please not smoke in my room?"

My Mama removed her hand from behind her back, bringing forth the Salem cigarette. She places it into her mouth, inhales, then blows the smoke into my face. I swipe the smoke away from my face as I fake a cough. "Ma, why you do that?"

"First of all, this is my house, and I smoke wherever I feel like it," she smirked.

I stand up. "That's why I cannot wait for tomorrow. Today is my last day in your house." I walk around her as I go towards the bathroom.

She follows me down the hall. "What do you mean? Are you moving or something?" It sounded like it was more of a demand than a question.

I stopped walking, and I turned around to face her. "Ma, I

THE DESTRUCTION OF FAITH

told you last month that I was moving out. You still do not pay attention to me."

"You have lost your damn mind speaking to me like this," she sounded.

"Ma, be careful; it's Sunday, and you are using curse words on the lord's day." My mother slapped me, and I fell back against the wall.

"As long as you are in my house, you will watch your mouth, and you will respect me," she shouted. She stood towering over me.

I glanced up at her as I held my face from her slap. It stung, and you would have thought I had gotten used to her slaps.

"Now get your ass up and eat that food and get ready for church. The bus will be here soon."

Slowly I stood up and looked at her. "I told you that I am not going to church." I began to feel a tingling in the back of my neck, and I knew that *she* was about to surface.

"You still running your mouth?" She slapped me again. This time I did not fall, but I stood my ground. That slap did not sting. I felt *Bella* was about to take over. That is the name I gave her after watching *Twilight*. She gave me signals and auras to let me know that she would take over to protect me.

"This is your last time hitting me." She went to strike me again. But, just as her hand came up in the air, the tingling in the back of my neck intensified. That was all that I remembered.

When I came to my senses, I had my right arm pressed against my Mama's throat, and my left arm had her pressed against the wall. She was clawing at my arms, trying to get me to release her, and tears were streaming down her face.

Immediately I let go of my hold of her, and she slid down to the floor, gasping for air. "Ma, ma, are you alright?" I cried.

"Get-the-fuck-away-from-me," she stammered.

3

"Ma, I'm sorry," I cried out.
"Don't you touch me again!" she screamed. She tried to stand up. I extended my hand out to help her, and she jerked away from me. I watched her stagger down the hallway towards the kitchen. I wanted to follow her, but I cried silently to myself as I returned to my room.

CHAPTER 2
MONDAY

TODAY WAS MONDAY, my moving day. I had managed to hide most of my personal belongings in my closet. I did not want my mother going through them and taking something that did not belong to her. My cell phone began to vibrate, and I picked it up and answered. The voice on the other end was my best friend, Stacey.

"Girl, you ready?" she asked. " I'm outside."

"Yes, let me say bye to mama." I hung up the phone. I gathered all my stuff and walked into the living room.

My mother was sitting on the couch watching the morning news. "Ma, I am leaving now."

Silence.

"Ma, you hear me?"

Silence.

"Ma..."

Silence.

She was giving me the silent treatment as she had done so many times before when *she* would come out. That had not been our first episode, and it probably would not be the last. But for some reason, she made everything still my fault.

My Mama knew that I had a second personality, but she ignored her and told me that I would outgrow it, but I never did. I named her *Bella*, and all I know is that she would protect me from the anger that my mother often released upon me. I remember the exact moment *Bella* entered me, and from that time, she has never left. *Bella* was always waiting around, hanging in the background, waiting to be released. "Okay, ma," I shook my head. "I will call you later."

Silence. I walked outside to see Stacey standing behind her car.

"Hey, sis," I said. I walked up to her and embraced her.

Stacey had popped open the trunk of her car, and I tossed my duffle bags inside the compartment.

"Why your face so red?" she asked me. She closed the trunk hood down, and as I got inside the car. She walked around to the driver's side and opened the door.

"My mama."

"Damn, I know that you are happy that you do not have to take her abuse anymore."

I glanced back at the house once again. I was hoping that she would at least walk outside and watch me leave. I wanted my mother to be that perfect mom and send me off with blessings and profound words to enrich my life on my new journey.

When it came to me, she was never gentle. I could never figure out why she hated me so much. How could you hate your child that you carried for nine months and abuse her so much? She often would tell me that she wished that she had been able to get rid of me, but I managed to survive her womb anyway.

Stacey climbed into the car, started it, and began to drive. As Stacey drove off, I waved back at that old gray house, knowing that I was finally leaving that negative energy behind. When we pulled up to the stoplight, a single tear rolled down my face.

CHAPTER 3
NEW HOME

I WALKED out of the leasing office, shaking the keys and laughing at Stacey. She waved her hands up and down in the car with excitement. "Girl, I am so proud of you!"

As I got back into the car, she reached over and kissed me on the cheek. "It is cool, ain't it?"

"Honey, cool is not the word that I would use for this joyous occasion."

"I know, but you know that I am not good with the vocab as you."

"So, where are we heading to?" she asked me as we pulled out the parking lot.

"Not too far from here. It's a small house located off Glenwood Avenue close to the pizza place."

"Just guide me in the right direction," she said as she drove the car onto the street.

I have always wanted to live on this side of town. I loved the big plantation-looking houses and the old feel of this area. The houses look ere very historic-looking, lived in by people with old money. Hell, even the high school looked like a giant castle. There was a history maker outside the school, and it stated that the school used to be the home of Sir Walter Raleigh. I know that there is a lot of energy walking around that place.

There was also an old movie theater within walking distance. It was the Colony Theater, and, on the weekends, it played old kung fu moves. But on the weekdays, it played classic black and white movies and musicals. I loved watching classic films, especially those dealing with the civil war, such as *Gone with the Wind* and *North and South*.

At times it felt like I had belonged in that period. Sometimes it felt like I was living in the wrong era, and it just captured my soul. I loved wearing those long bustling gowns and dresses. Even though it was an era of slavery, I imagined that I was Master, and the white people were my slaves.

We were on Glenwood Avenue, and I told her to take the next left before she got to the theater. As soon as we took that turn, my small two-story white wooden house stood between two huge brick homes. My heart began racing from the excitement of my place.

I loved my porch, for it encircled the entire perimeter of the house. My rent was only five hundred and fifty a month. The realtors told me that I would be paying half the rent for one year, a thousand a month. Maybe by then, I might have a roommate. But who knows because I needed all three of my bedrooms.

She pulled into the driveway and turned the car off. We did not even bother to get my bags out from the trunk. Stacey acted like she was more excited than I was. "Hurry up, open the door!" Stacey ran ahead of me to the front door.

"Calm down, chic," I said. I walked up beside Stacey and stood before the front door. I took the key and slid it into the lock. But before I could unlock the door, it just seemed to pop open on its own. It was as if the house had a mind of its own, and it was welcoming me in.

Slowly we both entered the house, and we stood in the middle of the foyer and glanced around its space.

"From the outside, this place looks so small, but this house is quite big," Stacey exclaimed.

"I said the same thing when I first was shown this place." I closed the door behind us. We began walking around the house. We both walked into the living room and noticed a vast copper color sofa up against the wall.

"Where did this come from," I asked.

"You did not place that here?"

"Nope," Stacey walked over to the couch and removed a piece of paper that Somebody had taped to the cushion. She began to read it:

Hi Faith! I want to say, welcome home. This couch was sitting in this storefront window downtown, and when I saw it, I knew that I had to buy it for you. Welcome Home, Candice.

"Wow, this was so nice of her," I exclaimed. The couch went well with the wood floor and the red brick stone fireplace. But I was going to take the sofa upstairs and put it in my bedroom.

"Come on, let me show you the rest of the house, then afterward we can go get my stuff out of the car."

Stacey followed me from room to room, examining the closets and the fireplaces. I had no idea why she kept opening the closet doors and peering all up into them. It seemed weird. I need to make sure that I ask her about this later. Each room except for the kitchen and the bathroom had its fireplace. The only room with carpet in it was the master bedroom, and I was good with that. I did not want to wake up with my feet touching a cold hardwood floor. The closets in the two bedrooms were large walk-in closets, and the bathroom was the size of the small bedroom.

"I love this bathroom," she said. She was staring at the

THE DESTRUCTION OF FAITH

bathtub resting on what appeared to be a lion's paws. It was an old tub.

"Me too. I immediately fell in love with the tub when it first caught my eye. Wait until I finish decorating this bathroom. You will be in love with it."

She followed me as I walked out of the bathroom and downstairs to the basement.

"Damn, this basement is big!" She went and stood in its center.

"I know. I have no idea what I am going to do with it, but I know that it will be a special room for me to vibe in." I had no idea what I was going to do with this basement. I had thought about making it become my smoke room or even a secret spiritual room.

"Your whole house will be a vibe that everybody will want to vibe in."

I smiled. "Except mama."

"Now, why you bring her up? You have spoiled the vibe," she laughed.

"She still my mama,' I replied.

"I know, but changing gears for a second. Did you go to the cemetery to pray for this house? I mean, did you go there and speak with the spirits?"

I smiled. "Yes, you know that I speak with the spirits there all the time. Why are you asking me about this? You know I have been going there since I was twelve. I was going there at first to escape Mama, but then the more went, I began to hear their voices sounding like whispers in my ears. The older I became, the clearer the voices came. So, yes, I will keep going to the cemetery to talk to the spirits for guidance."

"Well, you know that if your sanctified mother found out, it would be all over for those visits," Stacey said.

"I am grown now, and no longer do I have to report to her

about what I am doing." Saying those words, and hearing them come out of my mouth, were easier said than done. I knew that I never wanted my mother to find out about anything else spiritual that I was doing if it had nothing to do with the church.

"Well, don't worry about it, Faith. Let's finish bringing in your stuff," Stacey said as she began walking up the stairs.

We went outside and got the rest of my belongings from the car. There was a tall tree in the front yard, and I felt the urge to run to it and embrace it. I dropped my bags on the porch and did just that. I ran to the tree, and I placed my arms around the tree, holding it tight. I could feel its energy, and as the wind began to blow gently thru its branches, I heard a whisper in the wind.

Welcome home!

CHAPTER 4
THE BOOKSTORE

TWO WEEKS HAD GONE BY QUICKLY as my house was coming along. I had decided to go to the local black bookstore and buy myself a few books to start my library. I had only five paperback books, and they were dingy from being read repeatedly. The favorite of the five was *Dracula* by Bram Stoker. I was in love with the mythical creatures of the night. I knew each word of every passage that contained his dialogue. I want a vampire in my life. I even own the movie on DVD, and I can never get enough of the movie either.

My other four books were *Gone with the Wind*, *Roots*, *Grease*, and *Flowers in the Attic*. These books were special to me, for I got them from social service one year for Christmas. My mother could not afford to buy me anything for Christmas, so she went to social assistance for help, and they gave her a big cardboard box filled with stuffed animals. At the bottom of the box were those books. I did not care about those other toys; I just wanted to get my hands on those books and read.

I arrived at the shop based on the direction that Stacey had given me. She had told me that she often frequented the bookstore and that I would love it. I drove into the small gravel parking lot in front of the store and parked my car. Before I got out of the car, I began to feel a funny sensation, but I ignored it. What could be threatening me around here?

I walked into the small shop, and the first thing that awoken my senses was the sweet smells of smoke drifting past me from some incense. I noticed that there were three of them sticking out the dirt of a small flowerpot. I knew that I would make sure that a few packs of those would leave with me.

A tall, dark-skinned man with long gray dreadlocks wearing an orange dashiki stood behind the counter engrossed in a book. I closed my eyes and inhaled, and then I heard a woman's voice coming from behind me. I opened my eyes and turned around.

"Excuse me," I said. The woman smiled sweetly at me but did not greet me. I know that I had heard her say something to me.

"Pardon self, Queen. I did not mean to startle you. I was asking you if I could help you." she said.

"Oh, then my apologies to you. I did not hear what you said. I was too busy enjoying the aroma from those incenses."

"You like that scent? Well, it is called Egyptian Musk. I make them myself, but my husband tells me that they smell too sweet." The man behind the counter looked up from his book and smiled, then went back to reading.

"Well, I will take a few of those sticks before I leave. But I thought that I smelled Kush too. Anyway, I am here actually looking for some books to start my library. I want to find something that has to do with our people." I glanced around the store. "You have so many books here I do not know where to start."

"Start by telling me what you are interested in," the lady said.

"I am interested in everything," I replied.

"Follow me," she said.

I followed her thru these long red, black and green beads hanging down in the doorway. It had the seventies feel to it. Then we entered this open space which looked like a small community center. I noticed a small platform towards the back wall center, with a long curtain hanging from it. I could see the light flickering from candles hidden behind the curtain. The curtain appeared to be slightly moving as if there was a soft breeze passing thru it.

I watch her walk to a short brown bookshelf. She was wearing a long white dashiki with a white head wrap covering her hair. She was barefooted, but she moved as if she was of royalty. She reached on the shelf and handed me two books. One book was about how to establish an altar, and the other book was about African spirituality.

I took the books. "Why did you give me these? I am more interested in fiction books and or poetry books."

"You said that you were interested in everything," she answered.

I flipped the books over, reading the information about the knowledge contained inside. I have been experimenting with certain things. Especially more new age religions. I could never get with Christianity, for I always felt more for me than just church and their ways. Not only did I speak with the dead, but I could sense things about other people, and I had even taught myself how to read playing cards.

"I think you need these. I sense that you have a spiritual gift, and I want you to have these. I strongly believe that these books will help you to understand the ways of the Ancestors."

"The ancestors?" I said. It was more of a question than a statement. I knew about them, but I was not as knowledgeable as I should be.

"Yes, those great Africans that have come before us. It would be best to read those books to understand better the role they play in your life. Those books will also help you understand the role that you have to fulfill."

"I do not understand what you are talking about, but I will take these. I still want to see other books." I tucked the books under my arm.

"This is a bookstore, and you should read other books too. Feel free to look around my store."

She turned and began walking back out the way that we had come in as I followed her. She walked behind the counter and stood beside her husband. She was staring at me so intently. It was making me nervous, and I began to feel cautious. For some unknown reason, I did not have the urge to look at other material. I walked up to the counter and placed the books down. "I'll take the incenses."

"Only charge her for the incenses and not the books," she said to him.

"I do not know what to say," I said. I was grateful because I did not have that much money.

"Well, you just moved into your place, and I know that your money is minimal. Besides, you must remember that nothing in this life is free."

"*Wow, what does she mean by that,*" I thought to myself. "*What did she mean by that, and how did she know that I had just moved.*"

"Sistah, it will be five dollars," spoke her husband. He took the incenses and placed them into a paper bag. He slid me the books.

As I began removing the money from my pocket, I heard a rattling noise coming behind us. It sounded like someone had just walked thru the beaded doorway. I turned around to see who it was, but no one was there. The movement was like

THE DESTRUCTION OF FAITH

it had come from the direction of the area where we had just left.

"Is someone else here?" I asked.

"No, none is here but us." Even though she sounded overly sweet, I began to feel that she was lying to me. Someone had been watching us, and they moved those beads.

"Sista, what is your name?" she asked me.

You can tell me that I have moved, but you are asking me what my name is?

"Oh, I am sorry, my name is Faith Jones."

She bowed her head to me. "My name is Nana Madou. I want to invite you back on Sunday to our Akwasidae celebration."

"Oh, what is that about?"

"It's a ceremony where we call down the Ancestors to come and bless us with their gifts and presence," her husband answered. That must've been a grave mistake for, Nana Madou glanced at him and he, lowered his head.

"I did not mean to be disrespectful, my queen," he spoke, standing there with his head hung low, being silently scolded like a small child. Like he was interfering in grown folk's business.

She smiled sweetly at me, ignoring him. "So, will we see you on Sunday?"

I glanced over at him to see if he would raise his head, but it was still hung low.

"Okay, sure, but what do I wear or bring?"

"Wear all white and bring some liquor if you can."

I grabbed my bag off the counter, and I placed the books into my bookbag. The scent of Kush was still on me. As I walked out of the store, I thought I saw a young man standing in the shadows of the store.

CHAPTER 5
ALTAR

WHEN I ARRIVED HOME, I immediately dug the books out of my bookbag and took out the one that showed you how to establish an altar in your home. I got a smudge stick that I had bought at another store, and I used it to cleanse the space in my living room.

I was very much into spirituality, and I understood certain things existed in our universe. I knew that I had a gift to feel certain things in the atmosphere, but I had never created an altar.

The book instructed me to use a small table and place a white cloth across it. I had seen a small table upstairs in one of the empty bedrooms, and I went and brought it downstairs. I used the smudge stick to cleanse the table. I then placed a white cloth on it and walked into the kitchen to get a glass bowl from the thrift shop. The book instructed me to add cool water to it. After I did that, I placed a bowl of water on the table.

I began to gaze down into the bowl of water. The book instructed me to just gaze into the water until a vision came to me. I kept staring into that bowl of water for what seemed

THE DESTRUCTION OF FAITH

like hours, but it had only been five minutes. Just as I began to end this foolishness, I heard the whisper of voices. "What the hell," I spoke to myself. The voices became louder as I listened harder, figuring out what they were saying to me. The whispers started to become louder and more precise. It sounded like a rush of water in my ears, but I began to understand them.

"We have been waiting for you."

I dropped the bowl of water as it hit my table but did not break. I backed up from the table and ran upstairs to my bedroom. I stood there trying to figure out what had just occurred. My heart was racing, but what was more peculiar was that I was not feeling any tingling sensation in the back of my neck. I went back to the living room and picked up the bowl of water. I peered back into the bowl; I began breathing to control my heart rate. I was in my house, and I should not be afraid of anything in my home now. I heard the voices again, but this time I listened to the voices whisper my name.

"Faith."

Fuck that! I dropped the bowl again and ran back upstairs to my bedroom. I did not know why I was acting like I was so afraid of hearing voices. I listen to them all time when I visit the cemetery, but this was different. I never gazed into a bowl of water before, and I had never erected an altar to my ancestors either. I was alone in my home, embarking on something unfamiliar with, which was so different. I had no idea how to create an altar to my ancestors, and I needed guidance. Slowly, I removed my clothing, slipped on my Bob Marley t-shirt, and got into bed. I will take a shower tomorrow. I laid back against my pillow and closed my eyes. My thoughts danced around in my mind until I finally fell asleep, still thinking about the water in the bowl.

CHAPTER 6
VISITATION

I WOKE the next day to the sound of my cell phone ringing. I was slightly confused as I searched for it and saw it lying on the floor. I reached over and picked up my cell phone off the floor. I turned it over, and it was my mother. I pressed talk.

"What are you doing?" she said to me. I could not believe that she was calling me and asking me what I was doing. I was pleased to hear from her.

"Nothing, how are you?" I was hoping that she could hear the excitement in my voice.

"I'm fine; I need you to come over here today. I got something I need to speak with you about."

I guess she didn't sense it. "Well, if it is about what I said before I left, I am sorry."

"No, it has nothing to do with that. I just need to talk to you about something." My mother sounded very annoyed.

"Okay, ma, I will be there today." I hung up the phone. We never said goodbye to each other nor hello. What did she have to tell me? I had not spoken to my mother in almost two weeks and now she wanted me to drop by to see her. I had tried to call her to tell her that I finally bought myself a little

THE DESTRUCTION OF FAITH

car from Craig's List for about 600.00. It was a purple Volkswagen bug, and I loved that little car. It needed a lot of work, but it got me from one point to the next.

I wanted her to see my place and tell me that she was proud of me for having found something of my own, but she would act as if I owed her for sharing that information about my life. She probably would say something negative, for she had a knack of always turning my good news into something terrible.

Since I was sixteen, I have worked and saved every dime she did not take from me. I hated working at McDonald's, but it paid the bills, and my hard work got me a full-time position.

I was planning on going back to school to get my degree in Criminal Justice. I wanted to be a private detective for the defense teams and work with court-appointed lawyers. I guess you can say that I was an advocate for what was right.

I got up from the bed and walked into the bathroom. I turned the shower on to get the water hot and stepped into the shower. I allowed the water to cascade down my body as the water began enveloping me, and I felt so relaxed. I closed my eyes and leaned my head against the shower wall, and breathed.

Last night was crazy! Those voices were weird, and I knew that I was not playing games with myself by believing that it was only in my mind. The shower began to get steamy from the hot water, and condensation began forming on the glass doors of the shower stall. I wiped the doors with my hands. I blinked my eyes because I thought I saw someone standing there. I wiped the window again to see better, and there standing in front of me was this dark woman.

She was standing there with long flowing hair and scantily clothed. A colossal snake was hanging from her neck. I jumped back, startled, and then slowly placed my hand upon the glass to open the door. I could feel my heart racing, and my hand began shaking as I pushed the door open. No one was standing there. I walked into my bedroom with soap running down my body to look for her, but she was gone. It was like she had disappeared into thin air.

"*Damn, what the fuck is going on?*

Last night, I heard voices from the water I was peering into, and now this woman is standing there with a snake wrapped around her neck. I turned back around and walked to get back into the shower. Suddenly I stopped! Somebody had written a name on the glass; *Mami Wata*. I know that I am not going insane. I was going back to see that lady at the bookstore.

CHAPTER 7

MAMA AGAIN

I HAD no idea what my Mama wanted when I pulled up in front of her house. She was sitting on the front porch in that old white rocking chair waiting on me. I hated coming over here, but she had asked me. It is like you know how you beat a dog, but that dog will still come to you with love and protect you? That is how I felt about my Mama.

I walked up to the porch and sat down in the second white rocking chair beside her.

"Ma, I'm here. What do you want?" I asked. I was beginning to dread coming here.

"Girl, I have not spoken with you in two weeks, and I wanted to know how you were doing," she said.

I swear this woman can change hr mood at the drop of a dime. I glanced down into her small brown ashtray and saw a half-lit blunt resting there.

"You got a light?"

I reached into my bag and gave her a cigarette lighter. Things never change. "Ma, tell me what's up. I am tired, and I need to lay down. I had problems sleeping last night."

"Hmm, why are you so tired. You ain't got a job?" ma said, lighting her blunt.

I shook my head at her. "Ma, I been working since I was sixteen. You do not pay any attention to what I do unless it benefits you."

"Well, you never gave me a dime for staying here. You owe me back rent," she inhaled on the blunt.

"Ma, you were taking half my check. I can't believe you just said that." She was causing me to become agitated. "Is that why you call me over here?"

She blew smoke from the blunt in my face. It was as if she was toying with me. I was beginning to get impatient. "Ma, what you want."

"I wanted to talk to you about what you been doing behind my back. I know that you have been going down to that cemetery conjuring up all those demons. Stacey told me that she felt like you had ghosts over there."

Yes, I love going to the cemeteries because people do not follow you there and do not have to worry about ghosts. From time to time, I may have spoken a few words or written a poem here and there about the dead people there, but it was not her business to tell my Mama! I knew that I was not conjuring demons. What the hell was up with Stacey telling that lie?

"Ma, why are you still smoking weed? I thought you were going to quit," I said, trying to change the subject.

"Nope, and it's not a sin to smoke." Mama pulled on her blunt again and rereleased the smoke towards me.

I shook my head, "I never said that it was. What you want, I got things to do."

"What you be doing in that cemetery," She pulled on the blunt again. She slowly exhaled the smoke from her lungs. She was doing that shit on purpose. "Now that's a sin."

"What cha' talking about ma?" I had become exasperated.

THE DESTRUCTION OF FAITH

"You heard me; what in the hell do you be doing when you be going to that dead people place? Your friend Stacey told me that you are writing stuff that comes true that you are talking to dead people and then seeing ghosts and shit. You probably conjured up that demon that you got inside of you."

"And you keep smoking weed. Like what you do is none of my business and what I do is none of yours. Besides, I don't have a demon inside of me." I stood up, for I was ready to go.

"I hope that you ain't doing no witchcraft for the bible says suffer a witch to live."

"Is this why you called me to come over here? For once in my life, I thought you wanted to see me or wanted to tell me that you missed me."

"Yes, Faith. I called you over here because I am concerned about that demon inside of you. Now you got ghosts in your house, and you keep staying at that graveyard. I am worried about your soul. I do not want you to go to hell and burn in the lake of fire!" she spoke.

"When I was living here, you made me go to church every Sunday and three times during the week. Now you want to talk about my sins. What about the sin you committed when you killed my baby? I never wanted to have an abortion! You even tried to beat my baby out of me!" Tears began to flow from my eyes. I wiped them away with the back of my hand. I could feel my emotions rise, and the tingling in the back of my neck was beginning to start.

"You damn right I made you do that shit. You were not about to bring a baby in my house for me to raise. Is that why you have been to that place? You been trying to talk to your dead baby?"

I shook my head at her. I never thought about communicating with my baby. "You know, ma; I am going to leave." I needed to leave her and go calm down. I began walking off the porch.

As I started walking away from her, I heard her rise out of the rocking chair. "Where the fuck you are goin'!" she yelled. I felt her hands on my back.

She pushed me, and I almost fell down the stairs. I turned around to confront her. The tingling in the back of my neck was becoming more assertive, and I knew that I would, no Bella would hurt her if I did not leave. I turned around to face her. "Ma, that will be the last time that you will ever put your hands on me. The next time you touch me you -"

"What, you will kill me!" she screamed. "I am not afraid of the devil, for greater is he that is in me than what you got inside of you!"

Angered erupted from my eyes, but I did not give in to it. The thought of killing Mama had never entered my mind. I realized that it was time for me to forget about her and release all family expectations. I turned around and walked off her porch. I could hear her slinging curse words at me as I drove off.

CHAPTER 8
THAT DAMN STACEY

As I drove away from my Mama's house, I picked up my cell phone and dialed Stacey's number. Stacey answered like she had been waiting on my call.

"Hello, best friend," she said. She sounded all happy, but not for long once I finished telling her what was on my mind.

"I just left my mom's house, and she told me what you said." I was not in the mood for small talk.

"I knew she was going to tell you, but let me explain. I was not trying to put you down."

"Stacey, regardless of the circumstances, you had no right telling her what I did!" My voice had raised. I was shouting at her.

"Well, what you are doing is evil, and you need to stop," Stacey said.

"I guess it's okay when it helped your ass out, huh? I tell you what, lose my number and do not bother me again." I was interested in the spiritual world, especially the darkness, but I thought it was a phase I was going through. It did bother me to talk to her like this, but I was angry. She knew how I felt about my mother. That might have been the reason she was asking me all those questions when she had helped me move.

"Okay," she said.

I hung up the phone before she could do it first. I wanted her to feel how upset I was.

But then a thought entered my mind. I used to get invited to attend poetry slams, but that had slowed down. Stacey and I used to write poetry in school. I always thought that she wrote better than me. I would write, but sometimes I had this strange feeling that what I wrote would manifest into reality. There would be minor signs here and there. Finally, I began to believe that my poems had some power.

Once I wrote that this boy that I liked in high school would kiss me in my journal, and one day he pulled me into the auditorium and kissed the hell out of me. One time, I wrote that Stacey's pet dog would die for chewing up my favorite shoes during a sleepover. Two days later, the dog was found dead. Stacey was a great poet, thanks to me. I would tell her how to perform and not be afraid to get up on that stage. I knew that I could do spoken word better than she, but I was scared that my shit would come true, and I didn't want to hurt anyone with my words.

Fear held me back. People call her the *queen of poetry*, but I never read my poems aloud except in the cemetery. Maybe Stacey was going around telling people behind my back that I was a witch. My bond with spirits was more potent than my bond with people, and that is what mattered.

CHAPTER 9
BETTY

I SAT in my car watching the time on my phone. Faith had told me to be at her house around noon, and she was late. I kept glancing at the clock. My impatience began to show as I vigorously tapped on the steering wheel with my newly manicured nails.

When I had first met Faith, I did not like her. Faith was standing on stage beside Stacey, always acting like she was Stacey's bodyguard. Everybody loved them, but I hated Staccy. I believed that Stacey was just using Faith because she didn't have that much talent without her.

I felt that Faith had always looked so exotic to me. She kept the sides of her head shaved, and she always wore these long white locs. She had tattoos and body piercings, and I always thought she acted like she was better than everybody. I would glance around the club and notice how all the men could not keep their eyes off her. Faith pretended like she was immune to all that attention. I would wish that they would stare at me. What did she have that she didn't have?

One night Faith had recited a poem about rats, and the club began filling up with rats crawling all over the place, and when she said rats be gone, in one of the lines of her poem, the rats had vanished. But no one had paid attention to that manifestation. After Faith had recited that poem, she had walked over to my table and sat down. Her conversation was direct and straight to the point. Faith had stared at me for a minute, and then, she began telling Betty me about things in my life. I could not believe that she knew so much about me.

Faith told me that I keep coming to this club searching for my soul mate but never meeting him in the club. She told me that the man I was seeing was not the right one for me and that I needed to be patient, for the man of my dreams was coming soon. She was right. I was in this relationship with a guy named Greg. I believe I was more attracted to his good looks than anything else. But something was missing, and I was searching for someone else to fulfill that void. But Greg was so handsome, and I loved how we looked together when we would be out in public.

I had never met a woman like Faith before, and when I questioned Faith about it, she told me that she had been through many things in her life. Faith explained that she could communicate with specific energies, and they helped her with her gift. I was excited, for I loved the supernatural. I asked her whether she was born with a veil over her face. She answered me and said that she had no idea what that meant. I explained that sometimes children are born with a caul over their face, which gives them their third sight to see and speak with energies that other people cannot see. They are born with a caul over their face. The more Faith explained why I had made confident choices in my life, the more I began to like her. They say that you should not judge a book by its cover, and I had made that mistake by assuming Faith. That was the beginning of our friendship, and here I am one year later, still having her reveal things to still me.

I looked up into my rearview mirror and saw a purple

THE DESTRUCTION OF FAITH

Volkswagen pull up behind me. She told me that she would be driving a Volkswagon. The car was cute, but it looked old and needed work. Faith got out of the car and waved at me. I stepped out of my car and leaned against my Lexus. I watched her run up to me, and I was smiling so hard. I was beaming over with happiness to see my best friend making moves and doing things independently, but that car got to go. Maybe I am the bougie friend. I wish that I was in her shoes.

CHAPTER 10
FAITH

"I'm sorry that I'm late," I said, walking towards the house. Betty followed me. I was rummaging thru my bag, trying to find the house keys. I still had not placed them on the keyring with my car keys.

"It's okay," Betty said. I knew she was lying.

"Girl, stop lying," I laughed.

"Okay, well, you know that time is of the essence to me. I hate waiting. Cute car!"

"I love my car," I said to her. I knew it was cute, but it needed some work.

Betty followed me into my house and placed my bag on the hook next to the front door. She walked past me and sat down on one of the big pillows I had made. "When you going to get furniture. You know I got a bad back."

"I know, friend, but I am not thinking about that right now. It's cheaper for me to sew these big pillows and use them as chairs. Besides, the only people that come to see me are you and Stacey."

"What about your mom?"

THE DESTRUCTION OF FAITH

I took a seat beside her on one of the large pillows. "Do not mention that woman to me."

"Why do you hate your mother so much?"

"Where do I start. Let us see, my mother killed my baby, mentally and physically abused me. She stole and slept with my dead baby's daddy. Shall I continue?"

"Wait, what? Slept with your boyfriend? Damn, do not tell me anymore."

"Well, you asked," I stated.

"Never again. I thought my life was bad, but your life, girl...you never talk about your family, so I never asked. Are you the only child?"

"As far as I know. I have a godbrother who is in the military, and Mama worships the ground he walks on."

"Faith, all this time I been knowing you, and you have never exposed so much of your private life." Betty removed her shoes. She leaned back on the pillows.

I shook my head. "You know that when you ask me a question, it opens a door for another door to open up. Unlike most people, I do not like telling my business." I changed the subject. "What do you need from me today?"

"A reading, sis," she answered.

"Why do you need a reading? What's going on?" I asked.

"Nope, not telling you. I came here for answers, so you tell me," she smirked.

"Okay, sis, but do you want a cup of coffee or chai tea? The chai is cold, but it is good."

Betty laughed. "Cold chai tea? No, thank you."

"Well, let me grab a cup," I said. I got up from the floor and walked into the kitchen. I kissed the hanging vines that climbed across the top of the doorway into my kitchen. After pouring myself a cup of tea, I walked backed into the living groom. I opened the blinds. I wanted to allow the light from the sun to come in and warm my plants. I lit the candles that I placed all around my living room.

I believed that my house was my sacred space, just like my body. I wanted to turn it into a massive altar after reading those books. I did establish an altar based on how I felt, not what the book had instructed me to do. To me, every space in that house was sacred, which was one of the many reasons I did not allow people to visit me. I did not have the time to keep cleansing energy away from my home.

I removed my headwrap and took Betty's hands after I sat back down beside her. I felt a coolness come over me. I also sensed that Betty had a lot going on. I released her hands, and I grabbed the cards off the table and held them. I could not feel anything from them, so I placed them back on the table. I was going to just read her without them.

I like focusing on the person's energy and allowing whatever spirits surround them to speak to me. Everything must be natural with me. If she were not here, I would probably be in the nude. I walk around my house in the nude all the time. I do not like feeling constricted. I closed my eyes and began to focus on what I needed to see for her. I could feel a tingling sensation moving up and down my spine, and I knew that the message was about to come.

I often hear the name *Kalfou* in my mind when I am doing this. I had read about him on the internet, which spoke of him being a potent loa and that no one could hold his energy, but I believed that one day I would. I felt Kalfou around me, and then messages began to come to me.

"Betty, you need to start following the rules on your job. I am hearing that there are going to be some issues with your job. Do not get involved with none of your employees."

"Okay," Betty said.

"I am also being told that you are not happy with Greg

THE DESTRUCTION OF FAITH

and that he is not happy with you either. You know he is cheating on you. Betty, you need to get out of that relationship."

I could feel her emotions, and she was tearing up; I kept my eyes closed. "You are going to get a raise, so be thankful for it and do not tell anyone. But you will need to go outside and pee in the back of the building, asking for what you want. Urinating in the back of the building where you work is like placing something personal to you there. I know that I am jumping around a bit." I squeezed her hands tighter.

"Where are you hiding your bruises?" I opened my eyes because I saw them covered all over her midsection.

"What are you talking about!" She snatched her hands away from mines.

"You have been allowing this man to beat on you," I spoke calmly, but I felt my anger rising.

"No, I have not," she lied.

"Yes, you have Betty. Why are you lying to me?" I shook my head in exasperation. "My guides do not lie to me, and neither do yours."

Betty slowly raised her shirt, exposing burnt cigar marks as well as purple bruises across her stomach. I could not believe what I saw. I wanted to kill Greg for doing this to her.

"It just started, Faith!" she cried. She pulled her shirt down. "He's been going thru a lot with his baby mama."

I am so tired of her always making up excuses for him. I have been telling her the same thing month after month, and she still will not leave that boy. "You need to leave him plain and simple; I cannot believe that you did not tell me that you were going thru this? Why did it take for me to give you this reading to find out?"

"I'm sorry," she sobbed. "I thought you knew from all the other readings and was just not saying anything!"

"I looked at her. "They do not reveal everything to me. If you need a place to stay, you can stay here with me. I would rather have you here with me than live there with that beast while he keeps taking out his frustration on you." I moved over to her and embraced her.

"But he's cheating on me," she said thru her sobs.

Betty was beginning to get on my last nerves. You can lead a cow to water, but that does not mean that they will drink it. "Damn, is that all you can think about?" Betty nodded her head yes.

I pushed away from her. "Greg is beating your ass!"

"Stop yelling at me," she cried.

I calmed down. "Listen, I know that it hurts, but you got to listen. You need to leave Greg before you end up dead. I do not want to receive a phone call from a hospital telling me that you were brought in and did not survive his abuse. Would you please protect yourself and leave him? My house is open for you."

Betty covered her face in her hands and sobbed into them hysterically. I gave her a minute to cry it out, and then I got up off the pillows and went into the kitchen to get her a glass of water.

When I walked back into the living room, Betty was putting on her shoes.

"Where are you going?" I asked. I sat the glass down on the coffee table.

"I need to think about all that you have said to me. I will consider your offer but give me a chance to figure this out." She finished putting on her shoes and stood up.

I handed her the glass of water. "You need to think hard. I realize that you love Greg, but sometimes love is not enough."

"Thank you for the reading," she said, taking the glass

THE DESTRUCTION OF FAITH

from my hand. Betty drank the water and handed me back the glass.

"Hey, before you go, have you heard anything about me from the poetry world?" I was curious to know if she had heard anything. She handed me back the glass, and I could see that she was still crying.

Betty wiped the tears from her face with her fingers. She was very hurt, so I handed her a Kleenex sitting on the floor beside the pillow.

"Why, you ask?"

"Stacey told my mom that I am conjuring demons in the cemetery and that there are ghosts in my house."

"Are you fucking kidding me? Why do you still keep hanging around her because she is not your friend." She blew her nose.

"I think that too." I could see that she had stopped crying. She hated Stacey.

"Well, I heard that she was going around telling people that you were a witch and that they should not fuck with you because you be trying to steal their souls with your poems. Because your poems have some type of voodoo spell on them when you write them. People believe her because she reminded them of that issue with the rats. Girl, I need to get that baby oil because I am going to whip her ass!"

I sat the glass down on the coffee table. I could feel the tingling come into the back of my neck from my anger. "I need to calm down because I do not want to overreact."

The tingling began residing. "I am just going to see how this will all play out. You know, every time I am around Stacey and her so-called boyfriend, he can not keep his eyes off my ass."

Betty laughed. At least I had stopped her from crying. "Okay. So, what you are going to do. Sleep with him?"

"I'm going to see how this plays out. You know how I do."

Betty smiled. "Yes, I do."

"Good, you're smiling again," I said. Betty turned around and began walking out of the house. I followed her as I walked Betty to her car. I warned her again that she needed to leave him now before something horrible happened to her. I did not have the heart to tell her that I felt she would not be around much longer. I pray that I was wrong.

CHAPTER 11
EXPRESSIONS

I DROVE up into the parking lot besides Expressions, the spoken word cafe. It was First Friday, and the club was packed. Usually, Stacey and I came together, but I had been avoiding her lately. I still had not decided if I would perform this poem that I had written about the spirit that had visited me in my bathroom.

Tonight was First Friday the Cypher, and anything could happen. Every first Friday of the month, they would hold what was known as *The Cypher*. The people who ran the show would choose an artist who featured for that night. So much went on during the night. But what I enjoyed the most was the drumming circle. People would come as far as Charlotte to be a part of *The Cypher*.

I was glad that I had come early. I could get a great parking space. Usually, Stacey and I would be late, and she would have to park three blocks away. I am so glad that I have a car now, for I no longer must wait on a ride nor depend on someone else to take me around.

I got out of my car and began walking towards the club.

Three guys were hanging out near their vehicle, and I could smell what they were doing. I walked up to them.

"Ya'll be passing it to the left?"

One of the guys, who was very tall and I had never seen before, held the blunt.

"Why," he asked me.

I smiled. "I want to hit too."

He was staring down at me with his eyes quenched as if he were trying to figure me out. "What's your name?"

"Faith," I answered. He handed me the blunt. I took it and pulled on it.

"Man, this be the dark lioness, she be the dark goddess of this shit," spoke one of the guys that were standing there.

"Why do they call you that," the new guy asked.

"I don't know," I shrugged my shoulders.

"Stop lying," the other dude who was wearing a beanie said. "You be making shit pop with your poems."

I changed the subject. "You new to the scene?" I guided my question towards the tall guy. He was very handsome, tall like I said, and he had these strange tattoo symbols all over his arms. He was dark-skinned, with a low brush cut, and had gorgeous dark blue eyes. He also smelled so good.

"Yes, just here for a few weeks. My name is Freedom." I stared at Freedom, and I began to feel tingling up and down my spine. *That was very weird because I only felt those when I was mad. Was I being warned?*

I handed him the blunt back, "See you in the club."

"Fo sho, " he replied as I walked away from them.

"Damn, she must like you because she never speaks to dudes here. I thought she was gay cuz' she is always hanging around that chick Stacey," the beanie-wearing dude said.

I heard what they said, but I kept walking. Stacey and I played with each other a few times, but that was when we

THE DESTRUCTION OF FAITH

were both fucked up from taking mollies. I never looked at myself as being into women. I just liked what I liked.

I walked into the club and went straight to the bar. The bartender was a friend of mines, and she placed a red stripe on the bar. "Peace queen," she said, greeting me.

"Blessings Kim," I said. "I needed this."

I took a few swallows from the beer.

"I thought I would not see you tonight," Kim said while opening beers for another customer.

I took a few more swallows of the dark beer and placed the bottle down on the bar. "Why do you say that?"

"I heard some things. Somebody told me that you would not be reciting anymore," Kim said.

"Who told you that," I spurted.

"Look, I'm not trying to be in the middle of no shit. You are my girl, so hold it down tonight and know that I got your back." Kim moved down the bar to help the customers who were getting rowdy waiting on her to serve them.

I got my beer and moved to a smaller table. I glanced back over to the bar at Kim.

"She should have told me everything, but at least she was a good friend to me by warning me," I thought to myself.

I placed my bag on the table and pulled out my notebook. I began turning the pages to decide on what poem I was going to read. I started feeling a tingling sensation run across my forehead, and I began to feel negative energy. I started glancing around the club to see who was emanating the negativity. I reached into my bag and pulled out my mirror. In one of the books that I had read, that I had received from Nana Madou. It said that if you take out a mirror, you can use it to see what's is around you and investigate it; you can see if there is an evil spirit around you when you begin to feel negative energy. I had bought myself one from Dollar Tree.

I saw a shadowy red-figure near the club entrance, and I

put the mirror down. It was Stacey and her boyfriend and some other cat with them. Why did she appear red and shadowy? A question I would ask later to Nana Madou. I hope that I remembered even to ask her.

People were walking up to Stacey, hugging her and greeting her like she was some fucking queen. Usually, this never bothered me, but I could see how annoying she was since I found out she had been talking about me behind my back. I shook my head and went back to scrolling thru my notebook. I had written a poem about this water spirit, and maybe I would recite that. I needed the perfect one to read tonight.

CHAPTER 12
CONFRONTATION

STACEY GLANCED AROUND THE CLUB, searching for Faith. Someone had called her and told her that they had seen Faith driving a purple car. She had seen a purple Volkswagon parked outside, so she knew that she was in here. At first, she was nervous because she knew Faith was angry with her, but this was the first time she and Faith had not been to the club together. Like riding in the same car. Faith did not scare her, but she knew that Faith had darkness, which often made her nervous. Besides, Faith would not show out in this club.

"Boo, you want a beer," Marcus, her boyfriend, asked her. Marcus was from the Bahamas and wore long dreadlocks. All the women thought he was sexy, but to me, he was just like every other black man with dreads, dogs.

"Yeah, get me a corona."

"What's going on, Dutch and Duchess, Adam and Eve!"

They both turned around to see Judas standing behind them. He was the brother that had come in behind them. Stacey flashed a huge smile at him. She was secretly infatuated with Judas because he was at the top of his game in this spoken word world. Birds of a feather flock together.

43

"I was right behind you, but I was waiting for your groupies to leave." Judas was flashing those pearly whites at her. He was tall with long dreads and a long goatee. People often called him *Black Jesus*.

"Yo, you are blessin' the mic tonight," she asked him.

"I am the feature," he answered.

"Baby, I am going to get us those beers, " Marcus said. He walked towards the bar.

"I saw Faith's car outside; you see her in here," Stacey asked Judas.

"I did, but how do you feel about her being here?"

"I'm cool. I know that Faith is mad with me right now about speaking to her mom, but she acts like her shit doesn't stink."

"Well, you did do some foul shit to her, and you been talking mad shit about her. She is supposed to be your best friend, so you tell me how you would feel if it was you?"

Stacey frowned. "You act like you are taking up for her? You act like you are on her side."

"Yo, I ain't on nobody side but my own. Just be easy tonight and relax. I want nothing but positive energy around me tonight." Judas said.

I glanced up from my notebook again, and I saw Judas. He was the man that had walked in with them. That figures for he was always hanging out at their house. Judas was cool, but I always felt that he would turn on you at a drop of a dime. I reached over to get my bag, and I accidentally knocked my notebook on the floor. I stood up and bent down to pick it up. When I moved back up to get back into my seat, Marcus was staring straight at my ass. He had this dirty-ass grin on his face.

I was wearing some low-rise hip-hugging jeans with no belt, and every time I bent over, it would reveal the lioness tattooed on my lower back. I was wearing red thongs with a

THE DESTRUCTION OF FAITH

red bra to match my Bob Marley red, green and gold tee shirt. I smiled back at him. Stacey knew that he was a dog and that he loved staring at women's asses.

I grinned at him, and he smiled back. I stood up and sat bain in my chair. Seducing Marcus was going to be too easy. Stacey had a flat ass, but there was no way I would be with anyone so disrespectful. I knew that it made her feel insecure about her body, but he didn't care. I bet Marcus would love to find out about Stacey and me. He would probably want a threesome. Fucking dog!

"Hey, chic," Betty said, touching me on the shoulder, breaking me away from my thoughts.

"I thought you were not coming!" I exploded and reached over and hugged her. I was delighted to see her.

"I wasn't, but I didn't want you to be out here by yourself with all this drama." Betty sat down opposite me. I glanced over to where Marcus had been, and I noticed that he started walking away. He stopped and gave me that backward glance. I hope that Stacey saw him.

I turned my attention back to Betty. "I know that something is going on. Kim tried to tell me, but it was like she was warning me."

"Well, you know your girl is over there with Judas. Marcus can't be far behind."

I glanced their way. "Yeah, I saw that so-called queen come in the club. Shit, Marcus was staring at my ass before you walked up."

Betty looked around the club until she saw Freedom standing near the bar.

"Girl, it is some fresh meat in here tonight," she said.

I glanced over in the direction she was staring, and I knew she was talking about Freedom. "I know I saw that one outside. He is fine. Have you decided on whether or not you are going to become my roommate?

"Faith, please not tonight. I want to have fun and not think about him."

Freedom was staring back, but at me.

"Well, he is staring at you hard, and I think he likes you."

"Maybe his name is Freedom. I picked up on his vibe. He got some crazy energy, and he seems to be interesting. I did not pick up bad vibes from him, but something is going on with him."

Betty shook her head at me. "You need to relax and just enjoy life and love."

"I'm good. I do what I do, and it works for me. I love playing with both sides if you get my drift, and I do not need anyone blocking my lifestyle." I glanced back at the bar, and Freedom was no longer standing there.

"Are these seats taken?" Freedom had walked up to our table holding a six-pack of Red stripes. He placed them on the table. He startled me.

"I thought you were with those two guys," I asked him.

Freedom pulled the chair out from under the table and took a seat. He popped the cap off one of the beers with his keys and handed it to me. "Well, Joe got his thang going on, and the other two are chasing what I am chasing tonight."

"What are you chasing," Betty asked him. She reached for one of the beers.

I held my head down because I knew that he was talking about me. The tingling came back, and this time it was stronger.

What is going on?

"My sister is here somewhere, and she will be performing tonight."

"What is her name," I asked.

"Yemi," he replied.

"She's dope," I said. "I love her shit."

"You *are* speaking tonight?" Betty asked me. It sounded more like she was telling me than asking me.

"I might. Right now, I am just trying to feel the vibe."

"Don't stress, queen, for life is beautiful for you right now. Just relax and enjoy what is in store for you," Freedom said to me.

"Hmm, you act like you know something I don't," I smiled at him, and I could feel the heat rushing to my cheeks.

"Did I just make you blush?" Freedom took a swallow of his beer.

"Damn, he made you blush, " Betty exclaimed. She was laughing so hard at me.

"Stop it because I need to focus on what is around me versus what is good for me. Ya, dig?" I said to her. Freedom was smiling at me. He likes me.

"Yeah, I dig," Freedom replied. Now that sounded like it was a double meaning.

I smiled back at him.

"Excuse me, Faith, can we speak outside?" Stacey had walked up to my table with Marcus.

"I have nothing to speak to you about," I answered.

"Is this your new friend?" Judas asks, walking up behind Stacey.

"Yes, and who wants to know?" Freedom said, standing up. He was taller than Judas, and his presence seemed to dominate everybody.

"Wow, you did not tell me that you started dating." There was a hint of jealousy in Stacey's voice.

"What I do going forward is none of your business nor your concern. Now, do you mind stepping away from my table?" Stacey was causing me to get upset. "You do not have to make your presence known to me."

Betty stood up. Stacey glanced at Betty, then back at me. I

could feel that she was starting to become nervous, but she held her ground. "I want to talk to you," Stacey said.

"You heard what she said. What you deaf or something?" Betty had gotten all up in her face. Stacey backed away from her as I saw Marcus approaching from the left.

"I do not want any problems, maybe later." Stacey turned around and walked towards the stage, with Marcus and Judas following her like two lapdogs. Markus glanced back over at me, and I heard him ask Stacey who Freedom was in my life.

"Why do you worry about who she is with?" Stacey answered. Her face was full of hurt and anger.

"I thought she was a lesbian," he answered. I guess Stacey must have told him about our sleepovers. I saw him still looking at me; he wanted me badly. I sensed jealousy coming from him too.

"Naw man, I do not believe that she is a lesbian. I think she likes keeping her private life to herself. Besides, she used to give me the eye." Judas replied.

I laughed when I heard that because I had never looked at that punk. Yemi came to our table and took a seat beside Freedom. Freedom glanced at me, then excused himself. He had to use the bathroom.

"Peace queens, how you two doing tonight," she asked us, taking a Red Stripe from the carton.

"Hey, you cut your dreads off! I like the cut," I said to her. She used to have long locks, but now her hair was short, and it was cute. I did notice minor cuts on the top of her head when she took her seat.

"Thank you!" she exclaimed.

"We are good, but I didn't know that you had a fine ass relative," Betty said.

"Freedom fine? Sis, please," Yemi exclaimed.

"You are talking about me?" Freedom asked, taking a seat beside Yemi. He got to have Indian feet. Because every time

THE DESTRUCTION OF FAITH

he walks up, you never know he is there until he makes his presence known.

"*Damn, that was fast,*" I thought. This man was gorgeous, but I still could not ignore the tingling in the back of my neck whenever he came around me.

"He is visiting for two weeks. I'm trying to get him to stay longer, but he does not know yet." Yemi replied.

Freedom cut his eyes over at me. "Maybe I will stay a little longer."

We heard the emcee calling Judas up to the stage. The club had gotten crowded, and the show was about to begin. After Judas did his first poem, the club erupted in snapping fingers and catcalls. But then, when he started his second poem, I got up and walked outside. I was tired of hearing his voice. Judas always recited his lyrics as if he was slow rapping.

I saw a group of ladies standing near the fence laughing, and I walked over and sat down on the steps attached to the building leading up to the second floor. I closed my eyes as I began trying to memorize the poem I had written about *Mami Wata*.

As I close my eyes, I can see the smooth movements of the goddess Mami Wata, embracing my neck from behind as she tames the madness in my mind. I want to love her, no help her, but she helps me out of every situation fuck it! I cannot remember this poem, and I am just not with this scene anymore.

It seemed like every poem was written for clout and not about the message. The poetry the spoken word artist performed, not recited, no longer contained their emotions. Everyone wanted to be a star, and it seemed like they were competing against each other. Because it was the latest fad for some people, it was like no one was spitting that real shit anymore, but trying to have the appearance of being conscious, and they had no idea of what being conscious meant.

49

Hell, I did not even know what woke meant to me. But I knew that I was not down with this scene anymore. All my poems came from the heart. I often found myself writing about beings whose names I had never heard before. I did not understand everything, but I knew that when I spoke a poem out loud, shit happened! Pretty soon, I am going to stop performing for all these fake people.

"Can we please talk?"

I looked up, and Stacey was standing on the stairs in front of me. I had gotten lost in my daydreaming again. "Stacey, please," I pleaded. "What do you want?"

"I'm sorry for what I did."

"Okay, I get it. You sorry for telling my mother that shit, but what about for trying to discredit my name?"

Stacey smirked. "I am sorry for talking to your mother."

"You know, keep that fake ass apology. At first, I felt hurt because I was like, you are my girl, and we played with each other. But then, of course, the thoughts hit me that you were jealous of me, so I let it go. I thought that we were cool. I shared so much with you, and we had fun, but I cannot allow you to be in my circle again."

I stood up. "Can you please move so that I may go back inside?"

"Nope. I just want to tell you that I am the queen of poetry. I wear this crown, and you will never wear it. Yes, we had fun. But there is nothing that I need from you anymore. You are always acting like you know more than me. I see why your mother was always beating your ass!" Stacey stood in front of her with her arms crossed.

Now that hurt my feelings. I thought that Stacey was my best friend. "Stacey, I do not care about this. You go your way and let me go mines."

My eyes were pooling with water, for I did have a love for her. Stacey could see that she had hurt my feeling, and I thought I saw her wanting to apologize, but she did not. She saw those ladies looking at us.

"What gives you the right to speak to me like that? I came over here to speak to you, and you want to act like a bitch!" She was yelling at me, trying to make a scene.

I could feel the tingling in my neck get more robust, and then out of the corner of my eye, I saw a woman who appeared as if she were floating in the air. Around her neck was a giant black snake, and she was smiling. Then it hit me. She looked like the woman that had visited me in my bathroom. I could not believe that *Mami Wata* had called me and I wrote a poem about her!. The other ladies saw it, and they began to move towards the club.

"What are you talking about, Stacey?" I was trying to ignore *Mami Wata,* but she was moving closer to us.

"Is this your way of trying to keep turning others against me?" I pushed her to the side as I tried to get to *Mami Wata* before she could begin acting out on my emotions.

"You know what? You can burn in hell bitch!" she shouted.

I stopped walking and turned around to face her as I saw *Mami Wata* float above the stairs. She acted like she was about to remove the snake from around her neck. There was a loud crashing noise as Mami Wata's serpent flicked its tail and knocked all the furniture down.

The women ran into the club as Stacey stood there looking in fright, but she would not back down.

"Burn in hell? What you need to worry about is why Marcus keeps looking at my fat ass." I turned around and smacked my ass. My head was splitting.

Stacey went to swing on me. The pain in my head was fierce and squinched. It was unbearable, and that is when I blacked out.

When I came to, Stacey was on the ground with blood

coming out her nose, and the whole backyard of that club was in shambles. *Mami Wata* was gone.

"Faith, leave now!" the bouncer shouted at me.

"Why? I was out here sitting on the steps getting ready to ready to read my poem minding my own fucking business; when Stacey came out starting it with me, I begged her to leave me alone, but she kept pushing it!" I shouted back.

"Well, people came in the club yelling and screaming, saying that you and another woman was out here attacking Stacey," he said, calming his voice down.

"Yes, we saw it all, but where is that other woman? She was looking like she was floating in the air, and she had a black snake around her neck, " one of the ladies said. She had been one of those ladies standing outside.

"You know what, ya'll have this shit," I screamed. I began walking towards the gate in the back of the yard.

At that time, Freedom and Betty had walked outside. I saw Yemi walking with them.

"Faith, what happened?" Freedom asked me.

"I was sitting here minding my business when Stacey came out trying to act like she was sorry. I do not remember anything after that," I sounded. I was still agitated.

"Damn, it looks like a small whirlwind erupted out here, " Betty exclaimed.

Mami Wata must have done that, or her snake. She was protecting me. I was not about to tell them about the goddess. They would think that I was crazy.

I noticed how Freedom was remaining calm, but his eyes appeared to change to a lighter blue. Yemi stood there saying nothing, but she acted like she was taking a mental note of everything.

"Regardless of what transpired out here tonight, you know that we do not allow any fighting here. Faith, you are no longer welcomed in this club." the bouncer said.

THE DESTRUCTION OF FAITH

"Wait, What!" Betty exclaimed.

"The owners are not here, but I am going to tell you, Faith, do not come back!"

I glanced over to Stacey, and Marcus was by her side helping her up. Judas had walked out, and he was smiling.

Freedom came to me and took me by my hand and walked me back into the club to walk out the way I had come in. I walked past the populace as I tried to block out all their whispering; I held my head high as Freedom squeezed my hand tighter. The three of them, Betty, Freedom, and Yemi, walked me to my car.

CHAPTER 13
FREEDOM

WHEN I GOT HOME, I kicked off my shoes and threw my bag on the floor. I do not know what had happened because I had blacked out, but whatever did happen, Stacey deserved it. She had made it out to be like she was innocent, and I was the attacker.

I walked over to my small cabinet and removed a black candle, and lit it. I placed it on the small table by the front door. As I lit the candle, I bowed my head and began to speak to the goddess. "I ask that *Mami Wata* will close down the club and destroy everyone for not believing me."

I felt a coldness envelop me, and then I heard the hissing sound of a snake. I glanced around the room. I thought I saw the end tail of a black snake slither behind my door. I looked behind the door, and there was nothing there. My mind had to be playing tricks on me. I went upstairs and removed all my clothes, and fell on my queen-size mattress. I grabbed the vast army green blanket and pulled it over my head. I heard a soft knock at my door. The only person who would come over to help me would be Betty.

I got up and walked downstairs to answer the door. I

didn't even bother to put on something. When I opened the door, it was Freedom.

"What do you want? "I said with annoyance."How do you know where I live?"

"I followed you because I wanted to make sure that you were okay." He was grinning from ear to ear. I was nude, and I didn't care. I thought it was Betty.

"Yes and no." He could not keep his eyes off my body. I was thick in all the right places, and he could not take his eyes off me.

"Can you please put on some clothes?" he said.

"Does my nakedness make you feel uncomfortable?" I teased.

"A little, I did not come here for that, but to see if you were okay and to see you."

I laughed. "I'm at home. You are the uninvited guest, but I am making *you* feel uncomfortable. Just give me a second while I grab a t-shirt." I ran upstairs. I stopped and turned around. "...and close the door behind you."

I ran back upstairs to my bedroom and grabbed an oversize shirt, and slipped it on. When I came back downstairs, I went into the living room. Freedom had made himself comfortable on one of the big pillows. He was sitting beside my altar, which I had attempted to make.

"Can you please not sit close to that, " I told him.

"'My apologies, " he said to me. "My mother used to have an altar in her house for our Ancestors. Is this your ancestral altar?"

I sat down beside him. "I have never created an altar before, but this is one that I attempted to do, and when I heard voices whispering at me, it freaked me out." I gazed at him. I was glad that he had come over here. I knew that the tingling that I was feeling was *her* trying to come out, but I had to keep her at bay because Freedom had not done

QUEEN ZOAYA COUNTS

anything mean to yet, and Bella needed to calm down, I reached for the sage to cleanse the house, but I hesitated.

"What's wrong?" he said. He was watching me hard.

"Nothing. I was going to cleanse the house, but I'm not going to."

"Because she knows that I have good energy, and I am staying."

"She, what do you mean by her?"

Freedom started playing with the bracelet that he was wearing on his left wrist. "I thought you had a feminine spirit in here."

"Not me." I wonder whether he picked up on *her,* who lives inside of me. The tingling sensation had stopped, and I asked if she was feeling good vibes about him now.

I blushed.

"This is the second time that I have made you blush," he smiled.

"Yes, you are the first one to do so, " I replied.

"So, do you want me to leave now that I know that you are okay?"

"You get straight to the point," I said.

"Well, I know that you do not have a lot of people to come over here, so I do not want to wear out my welcome."

"And how do you know that? You seem to know a lot about nothing but everything." I watched him fidget around his bracelet again. What was up with that bracelet? Mental note to ask him later about that.

"No, please stay," I said. I hope that I did not sound like a jerk.

"May I remove my clothes and get comfortable with you," he said.

"You are asking me or telling me?"

"I am asking your spirit guides who I see moving around in here."

"Wait, What?"

"Faith, do you think that you are the only one who can see spirits? I see them all the time too."

"No, but-"

"But what?" he said, interrupting me. "I knew from the first time that I saw you that you were the one that they had sent me here for."

"Sent here for, what do you mean by that?"

"Faith," he said. He stood up and began taking off his clothes. "Well, they told me that I was going travel south and meet this woman who was going to complete me. She would possess a special talent, but she would be my person to help."

"I do not know if I am that girl, but I do know that I want you to stay." I could not keep my eyes off his chest when he removed his shirt. His body was so smooth like water. It was like he did not possess any bodily hair except what was on his head. I was becoming excited watching him remove his pants. He was not wearing any boxers, and he was very well endowed. I took off my t-shirt and got naked with him. Let's all get naked!

"It is a pleasure to see a woman that is very comfortable in her nakedness. Most sisters that I come across are often complaining about their bodies or are ashamed of their curves," He said, leaning back against the pillow and resting on his elbows.

I glanced down at his private part; he was not erect. But damn, it was already hanging large. I wonder what it looked like erect? "I love all my curves, even my potbelly, and the scar below it."

Freedom sat up and looked at my scar. "Did it hurt?" he sounded like he was so concerned.

"A little. I was pregnant, and I lost my son. I did not lose him, I was younger, and my mother took me to this lady to get an abortion. She did not do it right, and I began experiencing complications. My mother took me to the hospital. They had to remove my right tube and ovary. I still got my left side going on. For some reason, I always thought that my baby would have been a boy."

"Good, that means you can still conceive." Freedom sounded like he was excited that I could still have a baby.

I was beginning to feel uncomfortable talking about that experience. I needed to change the subject before I got upset again. "Hey," I said, standing up. "I got some mushrooms in my kitchen. Do you want to eat some with me?"

"I have never had mushrooms nor any kind of psychedelic drugs. I only smoke weed, and that is not a psychedelic drug to me. Why the hell not," he said.

I went into the kitchen and opened my cabinet door. As I began moving my spices around to get to the plastic bag which housed the mushrooms, I felt Freedom's presence enter the kitchen. I smiled. I could sense him watching my ass, and I began jiggling it a little bit. I felt him move closer to me, and I could feel his cool breath on the back of my neck. His manhood was barely touching my ass, but I knew I turned him on. His scent was driving me crazy. He was getting this tonight. I turned around to face him, and there was no one standing behind me. What the hell?

CHAPTER 14
MORNING AFTER

I WOKE up feeling very relaxed and incredibly pleased. I had fallen asleep beside Freedom on the floor. Stacey was no longer occupying the space in my head, but my mother's words were still lingering there. I stared up at the ceiling, watching the ceiling fan spin around. I knew that it was four blades, but I thought I saw eight.
I must still be high.
I had eaten about five mushrooms, enough to give me a little buzz, just a short trip. Freedom had never eaten them before, so I knew that I had to be the trip watcher with him. I needed to make sure that he would not freak out on me. But to my surprise, he had handled his trip very well.

It was kind of funny because he kept talking about being a god from the water and that he swam with the fish all the time. He had even broken down like a baby and cried in my lap. He told me that he had seen the spirits from the Congo. I had never heard of anyone taking a trip like he was having. Of course, I did not believe anything that he was saying. I just listened to him while he rattled on and on.

He told me that he saw a great spider crawling on the ceiling, which covered my whole top. I knew about the great *Anansi*, but I did not want to see her for real. What was she doing here, and what message did she bring? I try not to kill spiders, for there are stories that it could be *Anansi* bringing you a blessing, and if you kill her, you will lose your gifts. But I think it was real, for I woke up with a giant spider resting on my back. I tried to turn over but could not move. Then I heard a voice ask me to get ready, and I felt fangs bite into the back of my neck. But I thought it was just a dream.

I wanted to ask him about what had happened in the kitchen, and had he astral projected? I had read in a book and that you could do that. Maybe one day, he would show me if that had been the case. But Freedom just kept talking about water spirits and how they were more potent than any other spirit. I just listened intensely to every word trying to make sense out of what he was saying. I knew that it was just his trip that had them doing all this talking.

Finally, Freedom had collapsed on the floor, and I went and got a blanket to cover him. It would be a while before he woke up. I dozed off, watching him sleeping soundly. Freedom looked so peaceful, but I did notice that his eyes twitched a lot. I wondered what he was dreaming.

Even though I wanted to have sex with him, I was glad that we did not. There was just something about him that I wanted to see first. Besides, he caused a tingling in my neck, and that only happened when I was upset.

My phone began to ring, and I answered it.

"Peace is Freedom with you?" It was Yemi.

"Yes, he's sleeping."

"I was worried about him. I am glad that I saved your number on my phone. Glad that he is okay."

"No problem, I knew that you would use it one day." I snickered.

"Freedom likes you, and he is a good dude."

THE DESTRUCTION OF FAITH

"Yeah, I know, but I will chat with my spirit guides to find out myself."

Yemi laughed. I did not think that what I said was funny. I liked her energy. She was different from the other sisters that frequent the club. She always wore African clothes.

"One of the girls that were standing outside said that Stacey was faking, and she had asked them to be outside so she could set you up," Yemi said after she stopped laughing.

"I know, but I am glad that it happened. I need to stay away from that place anyway," I said.

"But who was the lady with the snake? She said that there was a woman out there with a big black snake around her neck. The way she described her it reminds me of *Mama Wata*?"

"You know about *Mami Wata*?" I asked. I was not surprised because of how she carries herself.

"Yes, where we come from, *Mami Wata* is worshipped heavily."

"Where do you come from?" I asked her. I thought she was from Raleigh.

"My family and I moved from New York years ago."

"Oh, ok, so up there, you all worshipped her?"

"It's not that we worship her; we work with her," she paused. "I think that I have said too much."

Freedom began stirring, but he didn't wake up.

"Oh, I did not know that. I heard the name and had seen a statue of her and decided to write a poem about her." That was not true. I wrote a poem about what I had seen in my bathroom, which turned out to be about her.

"That's interesting," Yemi said. The way she said that made me think that she knew why she showed herself to me. It was like she knew that I was not honest.

Freedom stirred.

"Freedom is trying to wake up. He keeps moving around," I told her.

Yemi was silent. I was sensing that she was beginning to get nervous. I hope that it was nothing that I had said. We were only talking about *Mami Wata*.

"Okay, well, tell Freedom to call me when he wakes up," she finally replied.

"Okay, I will," I said. I hung up the phone. Yemi had puzzled me a little bit. Towards the end, the conversation seemed a little strange.

CHAPTER 15
RUTH

FAITH'S MOTHER was sitting on the house's back porch smoking her Salem cigarette and drinking a cup of black coffee. She could not believe that Faith was a witch! She had tried to raise her daughter in the church with all her might, and here she was doing witchcraft. Faith was just so hardheaded.

She had gotten pregnant with Faith when she was sixteen and had her when she had turned seventeen. The social worker at the hospital had listed her father as unknown on her birth certificate. Ruth had been happy about that. She needed Faith's father to stay unknown. Her mother had kicked her out of the house, and Ruth had to live with her aunt. She learned from her aunt that she had to do whatever it took to take care of herself to survive.

At first, she was very skeptical about using men for money, but her aunt told her that nothing in life was free. To continue living with her, she needed to pay rent, and the only way to do that was to make men pay for it. She began to manipulate men by seducing them, and in return, they gave her whatever she wanted. Hell, she had a daughter to take care of and raise. Ruth loved Faith, but she was just not ready to be a mom. Her aunt had taught her well until the day she died and left her the house.

Ruth knew how to play the game. So, she did, and she was content until her friend Judy had asked her to go to church. At first, Ruth kept telling her that no. Ruth was not interested in going to church. How could she sit up in church knowing that she was out here prostituting? God didn't like ugly, and she did not want to be a hypocrite in the house of the lord. But Judy was very persistent.

She had finally agreed to go with her to church, and that day had changed her life. She had sat on the edge of her seat, listening to the preacher talk about fornication. The preacher would look at her a few times, and she just knew that he was speaking to her. Once he began speaking against sex as a sin when you are not married, the feeling that she had felt was worse than being molested as a child. It was worse than her enjoying those acts as she became older, and it continued for a few more years into adulthood. As soon as the preacher would make the altar call for all sinners to come and accept Jesus into their lives, Ruth had been the first to make it to the pulpit, and she joined the church. She had stood before the mighty God, crying and asking God to forgive her of all her sins.

But when Ruth got home with Faith, she would look at her daughter with disgust. Faith was a reminder of her past. She hated her daughter! She looked so much like her father, and it was hard for her to show Faith what little love she did have for her.

Ruth would constantly lie to her daughter about her father. She would only tell her how mean he was and that he was a pimp. Ruth told Faith that he had run off and left them. Finally, she said to Faith that her father had died in Chicago. Every time Faith would bring the matter up about him, she

THE DESTRUCTION OF FAITH

would change the subject. No wonder that child had a demon inside of her! She had been born cursed while trying to survive in the womb. Ruth had done all that she could to have a natural abortion, but Faith still came to be a pain in her ass. At first, she loved her daughter, her beautiful baby girl, but she began to resent her as she grew and looked more like her father. Ruth wanted to be able to have to stop abusing her, but it never ended. But then, one day, while she was yelling at her for not washing the dishes, Faith had fallen out on the floor. Faith was shaking and convulsing like she was having a seizure, and when she crept closer to her to see if she was alright, Faith stood straight up in the air and began attacking her. Ruth had not recognized Faith, but whatever was inside her daughter was calling her every name in the book, except the child of God. Ruth would back off, but she still did not stop with the abuse. It did not matter how much she went to church, Jesus was not saving her soul, and the abuse continued.

Ruth placed her cigarette to her mouth and inhaled. She exhaled the cancerous aroma, and the smoke formed a perfect circle in the air. It looked like an invisible halo. She laughed when she saw the ring of smoke. An angel she was not. As she sipped on her black coffee, she heard a loud knock on her front door. She got up from the back porch and walked through the house to answer the door. It was Stacey. What the hell did she want?

CHAPTER 16
STACEY

Ruth opened the door. "What are you doing here?" she asked Stacey.

Stacey was standing at her front door with her suitcases and tears in her eyes. "I need a place to stay," Stacey said as she gathered up her luggage and walked into Ruth's house.

Ruth shook her head and closed the door. *This girl is rude. I did not tell her to come in.* "What are you doing here?"

Before Stacey could open her mouth and speak a word, tears began to well up in her eyes, and they ran down her swollen cheek. "I left Marcus. I have nowhere to go, and I know that you got a spare room now that Faith is no longer here."

Ruth sat down on the couch and studied Stacey's composure.

"The girl was faking," she thought to herself. "Why did you leave him?"

"I found out that he was sleeping with Faith." She began to sob harder as she lied.

Ruth got up and walked her to the couch and helped her take a seat.

THE DESTRUCTION OF FAITH

"Are you sure that you got all the facts? Faith may be a lot of things, but she is good at being loyal. She loves you more than me."

"If you say so, but she did not tell you about the graveyard." Stacey saw a box of Kleenex on the coffee table and helped herself to a tissue to wipe her eyes.

Ruth nodded her head as if she were contemplating what Stacey had just said.

"She did it to get back at me for telling on her." Stacey wiped the tears from her face with the Kleenex. Then she continued. "But to end it all, last night at the club, Faith and I got into a huge argument. And then she turned into this monster I do not know what to call it. But whatever it was, it attacked me!" she glanced over at Ruth to see if she was buying her act.

Ruth could not believe that the demon had been let loose on Stacey. Faith was out of control, and she knew that she had to do something before she hurt someone else.

"I'm sorry, Stacey, that you had to go thru this."

"Why are you apologizing? Faith is the one that did this to me. Look at my cheek where she punched me. It's swollen! She just pure evil walking and talking!" Stacey was playing on Ruth's emotions.

Ruth stood up and went to the kitchen; she was smoking another Salem when she came back. "Ok, you can have her room for now, but we got to figure out what to do about Faith."

"Okay, Miss Ruth, thank you so much. I promise I will not tell her that I am staying here because if she found out, she would kill me."

Stacey had put on the best performance in her life. She had Ruth believing in whatever she told her about Faith.

"No worries," Ruth said, comforting her. She picked up

Stacey's suitcase and began walking down the hall. She took it into Faith's old room.

Stacey walked behind her, a smugness written all over her face.

"You been here so many times, so I will not tell you to make yourself at home," Ruth said, setting the luggage down on the floor. She walked over to Stacey and embraced her. She kissed her on the cheek then left the room.

As soon as Ruth had left, Stacey walked over to Faith's bed and fell backward onto it. She removed her cell phone from her back pocket and texted Marcus. *"Be home in a few weeks. I love you!"*

CHAPTER 17
THE MORNING AFTER II

I WAS FINALLY able to wake back up. I had fallen back asleep after Yemi and I's conversation. I reached over to touch Freedom, but he was no longer lying beside me. As I stretched, I saw Freedom, and he was gazing out the window.

"Oh man," he said.

"What you oh manning about?" I asked him.

"Was I acting crazy last night?"

"Hell, yeah, you were," I said as I laughed.

"I only remember bits of pieces of my trip." He turned around to face me.

"You did a lot of things. Saw a lot of things too, like spirits walking thru my house and *Anansi* on my ceiling."

I got up from the floor and went into the kitchen. We needed to drink some water. I removed a bottle of alkaline water from the shelf and handed it to Freedom. Freedom took the bottle from me and drank all thirty-two ounces down in one gulp.

"Drink water much?" I asked.

Freedom laughed. "I do not mean any harm, but that was

the first and last time that I will ever do mushrooms. I will stick strictly with the herbs."

I smiled. "People always say that, but you will do it again."

"No, I won't. Trust me when I say that I finished with something I finished." Freedom handed me back the empty water bottle. "Do you recycle?"

"Nope."

"You need to start because you should see all the pollution we got in our water," Freedom said.

The way he sounded, you would have thought that he lived in the ocean. I just stared at him.

"Well, try to recycle when you can," he finished.

I shook my head up and down to let him know that I would. "Oh, by the way, Yemi called, and she was looking for you."

"Shit, I left my phone in the car," he said.

"I told her that you were asleep."

"Good, I know that she was apprehensive about me."

"She said just to call her later."

"Can I ask you a question?" Freedom changed the subject on me.

"Yes," I said. "But let me sit down." I sat down on one of the pillows, and he followed me.

"Did we mate last night?" he asked.

"Mate," I chuckled. "No, we did not, mate."

"Oh, okay," he said. He sounded relieved. He sat back down on the pillow.

"As much as I wanted to fuck you last night, I did not take advantage of you."

Freedom was staring at me so hard that I thought he was upset with me for not taking advantage of this situation.

"Faith, can I be honest with you?"

"Sure," I said. The tone of Freedom's voice was making me nervous.

THE DESTRUCTION OF FAITH

"I am only here for a short time. I do not want to start something with you that I cannot finish."

I began to feel like I was about to get that friend speech, and we did not even fuck. Maybe I should have taken his manhood.

"It's cool," I paused. "You know what? I think that you should leave because I have a lot to do today, and besides, I do not want Yemi calling here again looking for you." I needed him to leave because I was digging into him, and I did not want to hear him tell me that he was not interested in me. As I stared at him, he looked puzzled.

He got up from my floor and slipped on his shirt. As fine as he was, he probably went around hurting women. I began to feel that tingling sensation come back.

Not now, Bella!

When I looked back at him, he was fully dressed. Freedom began putting his shoes on. He did not say a word to me. I waited for him to finish, and then I hurriedly walked him to the door, for I knew I was becoming offended and had no idea why.

Freedom walked out of my house without saying a word to me. Now, who had offended whom?

CHAPTER 18
FREEDOM

FREEDOM WALKED into the bookstore and went straight to the back of the store. He was hoping that Nana Madou would not come at him with so many questions his night. He was just visiting and what he did with his time was his business with no explanations needed. He knew that his visit was short, and he had to accomplish his goals. His thoughts were entirely on Faith, and he almost didn't see them. Yemi was sitting there with a book in her hand, and Nana Madou was lighting candles.

Let's get this over with, he thought to himself.

"Did you have fun last night?" Yemi asked as she glanced up from her book and spoke to him.

"Yes, I did," he answered. He walked over to Nana and kissed her on both cheeks.

"Have fun with whom?" Nana said to him.

"He-," Yemi started to say.

Freedom cut her off. "I had fun at the club."

"Ok, good to hear," Nana replied.

Yemi gave him a menacing look for cutting her off.

"I got the candles lit for you. I just did not pour libation

THE DESTRUCTION OF FAITH

yet. Do you mind if we skip that part?" Nana said.

"Yes, of course," Freedom replied as he moved towards the altar.

A white sheet hung up between the small stage and an earthen pot painted blue. Nana worshipped the water spirits, and the earthen pot belonged to one of the water deities that worked with her. *Asuo Geybi,* the water god.

Freedom glanced towards the sheet-like partition and removed his shoes. He walked behind it, knelt in front of the earthen pot, and began chanting.

Yemi placed her book down on the chair and walked over to her mother. She waited patiently and watched her mother light all the candles surrounding the altar. Once her mother finished, they both moved over to the altar and knelt on their knees. Yemi closed her eyes and took her mother's hands. Nana Madou held them tightly as she closed her eyes as well. They began to chant softly to each other. Yemi started to speak with her mother using telepathy.

"*I felt strange energy last night. What happened at the club?*" Nana inquired,

"*The girl that came in here was at the club. I spoke to her. I know her, but I didn't know that she was strong with the spirits. Mami Wata appeared. She is stronger than we thought,*" answered Yemi.

"*This is good news, for you can befriend her more and gain more of her trust.*"

"*I know, Nana. I do like her as a person. So, gaining more of her trust will not be a long process to do.*"

Nana Madou squeezed her hand tighter, and Yemi winced from the tight grip. "*Did Freedom stay with her last night, and please do not lie to me.*"

"*Why don't you ask him?*" Yemi thought.

"*Do not be disrespectful. When I ask you a question, you need to answer me.!*"

"*Yes.*"

73

"Did they mate?"

"No, Nana, they did not mate," Yemi answered.

Nana smiled at the good news. She stopped applying pressure to Yemi's hands.

They both released their hands from each other as they felt a cool breeze enter into the center. The white sheet began flapping as if something a wind was moving it, and they fell flat on the floor prostrating themselves to spirit. They both heard the earthen pot move. They looked at each other and smiled.

Freedom had read their thoughts, and he knew that Yemi had no other choice but to answer her mother. He loved the sincerity that Yemi possessed, but Nana was another matter. He finished what he was doing and moved away from them. He needed to rejuvenate.

CHAPTER 19
AKWASIDAE

SUNDAY CAME SO FAST for me. I had gone thru Saturday with no thoughts of my mother nor Stacey. I could care less about either of them. I guess Freedom occupied my thoughts as he stays on my mind constantly. It is like the last song you hear; you keep singing it until you hear something else. That is how my thoughts were of him, everlasting until something else could happen to distract me from thinking of him.

I had not heard from Freedom since he left my house on Saturday morning. Maybe it was better that way, for he was only in town for a few days anyway. I could not allow myself to get all caught up in his looks. Besides, I was not ready for love, and I didn't have the time to give to anyone. Love was not a word that I used a lot in my vocabulary, but I was thinking about that word with Freedom. Wow! What did I have that thought? I was not ready for anything that anyone had to offer.

I was still young, dammit, and I had all the time in the world to worry about that shit later. I enjoyed what I did with who I did with it, and that was that. These days they had a term for that; polyamorous. I place my thoughts back to the matter at hand, going to this stupid Akwasidae celebration at the bookstore. I regret the decision that I had made to attend. But, I needed to know why I heard those voices, and I needed to know what they meant. I should never have allowed it to spook me out like that. I can see shit and manifest shit thru my poetry, but to hear voices from gazing into the water, now that was crazy.

    I opened my closet doors, trying to find anything white to wear. Nana Madou had said that I needed to wear either all white or blue. I had a long white cotton summer dress in my closet, and I pulled that down. I wrapped my hair in a blue scarf and made my way to the bookstore.

    When I arrived, I had to find a place to park my car. This place looked crowded. I could not find a parking space in the small parking lot in front of the store, so I parked a block away on the street. There were so many people here. I was not ready for a crowd, but it was a festival. I glanced one more time in the mirror to make sure I looked straight, then I got out of the car and walked to the store.

    When I got there, I opened the doors to the bookstore and entered. I could smell the same scents as before, but the energy felt different. A few sisters were lingering around browsing thru the books and speaking amongst themselves. They were all wearing African attire with multicolored head wraps. That seemed odd to me because Nana had told me to wear either blue or white. Maybe they were just in here to purchase a few books and check out the vibe like I had done when I had first visited.

    I began walking towards the beaded doorway, and as I moved past the sisters, they all stopped speaking to each other and fixed their eyes on me.

    Why are they staring at me?

THE DESTRUCTION OF FAITH

I pushed open the beads and stepped thru the doorway. The moment I stepped thru the doorway, it felt like I had passed thru a portal. I know it is so strange to imagine, but I felt like I had entered a whole different world that I never knew existed. It felt like this was going to be the beginning of my life, my new life. The energy that I thought I knew or at least had little knowledge about was leaving me, and something was beckoning me to this life. Even if I wanted to turn around and run, I could not escape the feeling of belonging that was overpowering me.

Candles dimly lighted the room with dancing flames that seemed to cast shadows and silhouettes of the people I had never met. I could smell the scent of Frankincense and myrrh, and it was overwhelming to my senses. It felt like my third eye was opening to me, and whatever gift I possessed was being magnified by those sacred scents. I began to understand why the three wise men had offered them to the baby Jesus at his birth. They were heavenly scents, sacred to those born with a special gift to see those things that others could not see.

I glanced down on the floor, and I noticed a pile of shoes resting against each other. I removed my shoes and fully entered the room. Once again, a story in the bible entered my mind that I had learned in Sunday school. When God spoke to Moses and told him to remove his shoes because he was on holy ground, this was how this place was making me feel when I removed my shoes.

If I had to guess, about fifty people were sitting in the gray metal chairs placed in a semi-circle. They were all wearing African attire as well. All the sisters wore head wraps, and I noticed that I was the only one wearing white and blue.

What the hell is going on?

I looked up ahead of me, and I saw a white covering

hanging down from the ceiling and touching the floor. The material was cotton, but the way the place was all lit up, I could see the silhouette of a vast earthen-like pot sitting in its center. The people were speaking in soft tones, and it sounded like the whispers of voices that I heard in my house when I had spoken into the glass of water. Maybe that was a foretelling that I had encountered to tell me that I would listen to these voices. But the oddest thing about the people whispering amongst themselves made me think they were speaking about me.

I saw an empty gray metal chair to the right side of me, and I walked over there and took a seat. I wanted to stay in the back and just observe what was going on. Even when I would go to church with my momma, I would always sit in the back in the church and watch her take a seat in the front row pew, acting all dignified, as if we rode in a Cadillac to church while all we did was ride that blue bus.

There was a door towards the left side, and I saw six brothers walk thru that door, each carrying a Bantu drum. *The drummers!* Now that was exciting because I always wanted to go to an actual drumming ceremony. I had seen them on television, but now I was about to experience this in real life. They walked over towards six empty chairs sitting in front of the white veil.

Yes, that is what I will call that white covering because it looked like a white veil! Why did I not think of that before when I first saw it. It reminded me of a movie starring Eddie Murphy, who was trying to save a Chinese boy. The woman working with him took him to this holy place to speak to this goddess. She was hiding behind a veil, and when he snatched it down, she had the upper body of a woman, but her lower torso was that of a serpent. I wondered what was hiding in that earthen pot.

THE DESTRUCTION OF FAITH

Suddenly the room fell silent as I saw Yemi and the man who worked behind the counter walk thru the same door as the drummers carrying a large wooden stool. They placed the seat directly in the center of the veil. I was surprised to see Yemi here. But as I stared at her and him, I noticed a resemblance. Could she be their daughter?
I wondered why I had not noticed this before?
Yemi never told me that her parents owned this place. Well, I never asked. I was beginning to feel a little weird about being at this festival. She resembled Nana but looked more like *Baba*. That it was, I called him. I do not even know where that name came from because I had never heard of that word *Baba*. Later I was to find out that it meant father. They both took a seat beside each other.

I began looking around the room as my heart began to beat a little faster in anticipation that Freedom may be here, but I did not see him. I relaxed and brought my focus back to the veil. I heard a small bell ring, and this beautiful sister walked out thru that door dressed in all white and blue. Nana had followed her into the room. The people sitting in the chairs all dropped down on one knee and bowed to her. I just sat there because I had no idea what they were doing.

Nana Madou looked royal as she cascaded into the room wearing a long water blue gown flowing way down past her feet. If I had known any better, I would say that she looked like she was gliding with her feet two inches above the floor. Her head turned, glancing at the people. She saw me and bowed her head, giving me recognition. I did not know what else to do, so I got down on one knee and did as everyone else had. Nana glided over to the stool and took a seat.

Seven sisters were sitting in the front row, and they all stood up and moved to the veil, then turned around to face us. Nana reached under the stool and pulled out a wooden bowl covered in carved symbols. I noticed a massive bird carved on the front of the bowl, with its head turned backward but flying in the opposite direction. One of the women who had stood up handed her a bottle of gin. Nana stood held the bottle up over her head. She began chanting in a language I did not know.

"*It must be African,*" I muttered to myself.

The people were still on their knees as she began pouring the gin into the bowl. She was saying these names out loud. Later I would know that she was calling the attention of the spirits around her. Nana commanded that everyone call on their ancestors. I began hearing the people speaking the names of their dead relatives. I only knew two people who had died, but I was not going to call them, so I kept my mouth closed and listened. Later, I discovered that they were pouring libations to their ancestors and the African gods.

Once Nana was done, she motioned for the people to get up and take their seats. I got up, took my seat, and kept observing and trying to follow whatever they did to ensure I did not feel out of place. Nana sat down, and she began motioning the seven women to start singing. They were singing in the same African language that she had spoken in. The drummers began beating on the drums slowly until they caught up with the rhythm of the singing. I began to feel a tingling in the back of my neck, but it felt different. Not coming from anger, but more like something was coming my way.

I saw several of the people get up and walk towards Nana. They bowed down to her and then walked to the drummers and bowed to them. Someone had cleared the middle of the circle to provide space within the semicircle, and they began dancing in that space. They were moving counterclockwise within that circle to the beat of the drums. More people began to follow them, and I was in awe as I saw them dancing

THE DESTRUCTION OF FAITH

and spinning around in that circle. When they got tired, they would go back towards the drummers, bow down to them by touching the floor with their fingers, and then to Nana repeating what they had done in front of the drummers before going back to their seats.

Nana motioned to the seven women again, whom I take to be her singers, and they switched up the song. The drummers started slowly again, and the crescendo of the beat became faster. I saw Yemi get up and bow down to them as well and head straight for that circle. She started moving in that circular space. She was dancing fast, not missing a beat, and she twirled and spun around. It looked like she was turning in the air at times. The tingling increased in the back of my neck, and I began to shake. What was happening to me because I had never had this experience before. I wanted to get up and dance with her, but it felt like something was trying to hold me down in my seat! I wanted to dance so badly, but I could not rise out of my chair to join her.

The energy became intense, for every time she spun around in that circle, the tingling in the back of my neck hit me. I closed my eyes, trying to fight that urge to dance or try to fight that feeling, but something was overtaking me. I grasped the side of the chair with my hands as I gripped it tight to make myself be still from the shaking and trembling that was happening to me. Whatever was trying to take me was hurting the back of my neck. It was like my protector and something else were fighting each other and that something else was more potent than what was inside of me.

I had this feeling of being pulled into two separate pieces. I was shaking so violently that I thought I was going to have a seizure. My head felt like it would explode, and I could hear rushing water in my ears. It was overwhelming as the sound became louder and louder, and I could not take it anymore. I heard a scream. I turned my head to see where it was coming from, only to realize that it was me. Whatever had won the fight was speaking in that African language, but the shaking had not stopped.

Another loud yell escaped my mouth as everything went black; the rushing water filled my head.

CHAPTER 20
POSSESSION

I SLOWLY OPENED my eyes and heard people shouting in my ears. They were asking me for a name. My locs were hanging in my face, and my headwrap was on the floor. I looked down at my feet, and Nana was down her knees, bowing to me.

What the hell? What had just happened?

Nana was extending her arms out to me, and she was handing me her beads from around her neck. I glanced down at her, but I was still shaking. I began to look around the room slowly, and I was now sitting on the stool. How did I end up here? What the hell was going on? What had happened to me.? Why was she on her knees? I tried to open my mouth to speak, but the sounds coming from my mouth were just hoarse and raspy mutterings. I heard this male voice tell me to just be quiet for now. It sounded familiar, but I was not in the frame of mind to determine where I had heard it.

When Nana realized I was looking at her, she stood up and placed her beads back around her neck. When I looked down at myself, I saw that someone had covered my lap in this blue cloth. I reached up to touch my face, and there was white powder all over my fingers when I drew them back. I glanced around the room in confusion. I was perplexed at all that had transpired. Everyone was staring at me with looks of bewilderment as well as cautiousness. I tried to stand up, but my legs felt wobbly, the blue cloth in my lap fell to the floor, and one of the singers immediately picked it up. I sat back down.

I glanced towards the veil and saw a huge white cloth resting on the floor, where people had placed their offerings. I saw plantains, bananas, sweet potatoes, pineapples, and liquor bottles.

I had not seen that placed there earlier. Then it hit me; I understood why Nana had told me to bring those items. They were offerings for the spirits. Some things were making sense, but yet I still felt like I was in confusion.

I tried to stand up again, and this time I felt the strength in my legs returning. I was not as shaky as before. The drummers were no longer beating on the drums, and the singers were no longer singing. Yemi was standing near me, and I felt a little safe. The people screaming in my ears had moved away from me and were now sitting in the gray metal chairs watching Nana and me.

I tried to focus more on everyone's faces as the room seemed brighter to my eyes. I could smell Freedom's scent. I was looking around the room for him, but he was not there. Maybe this was not his thing. Perhaps someone else wore that fragrance. Nana turned to face the crowd, and she raised her right hand to the air and twirled it around. Nana commanded these people with such grandiosity, and they did whatever she told them to do.

The way she stood over them made me think that I was in church, benediction from church. Someone had turned on the lights, and the people stood up. Nana spoke in that African language again, and they all began socializing with each other.

THE DESTRUCTION OF FAITH

Please, do not let this be like church.

"Are you okay?" Yemi asked me, walking up to me.

"Ye-yes," I stammered. My voice was still raspy, but I was able to speak again. "What happened to me?" I said.

Nana turned her head to me. She placed a finger to her lips as if to tell me to be quiet. I did not like that, but I did not feel any anger. Usually, when someone would offend me, that tingling would arise, but I did not feel it. What the hell? Yemi told me to sit back and be patient.

"All your questions will have answers soon," she said.

Suddenly I saw a tall shadow of a man standing near the veil. It looked like Freedom, but when I blinked my eyes, it had disappeared. Damn, I must be losing my mind. I could not remember what had happened, like the episodes that I had with Bella. But she saw Nana look in that direction as well. I had no idea what had happened to me, but someone was going to tell me something!

CHAPTER 21
FREEDOM

FREEDOM KEPT WALKING IN CIRCLES, becoming impatient as he waited for the door to open so that he would be able to join the others. Being at the bookstore provided him with the necessary energy to get him through his day. The air was always smelling different scents and charged with the large crystals Nana kept in certain store corners. Freedom was so excited about this festival that was taking place today. He was very anxious to see Faith most of all. He had not called her since he left her on Saturday morning. He wanted her to have her space, and secretly he was hoping that she would have called him.

Freedom had to remember that this was not the olden days where men had to be the ones to court the women that they wanted. The periods were different now, and if she wanted to speak to him, she could have reached out. But then he had told her that he was not looking for anything nor anyone. Freedom heard the door to the front of the store open, and he saw Faith walk in. He remained hidden behind the shadows, watching her move about the store. She looked so beautiful, dressed in white clothing and her

THE DESTRUCTION OF FAITH

hair wrapped in that beautiful blue cloth. It was water blue, dark blue like deep parts of his eyes. Blue was his favorite color.

He kept his eyes on her as she entered the center, and he noticed all her facial expressions and body movements. He could tell that she was excited, but some nervousness had shown in her eyes simultaneously. He had experienced where others unfamiliar with the culture would be nervous the first time, especially if they came from a church background.

Freedom wanted to go to her, but he knew that the time was not right, not yet. He watched the drummers walk out and take their position as Nana prepared for her grand entrance. It was always a pleasure to watch her enter the room. She carried so much energy with her that the room seemed electric every time he saw her. He did enjoy the Akwasidae celebrations that she held for the ancestors.

Yemi looked just as grand when she had entered with her father, but she was not on Nana's scale. She still had a lot of growing to do in her own right. Freedom envisioned himself as being like Baba, Nana's husband. Baba often remained laid back and incognito. Just sit back and allow the women to handle things. Freedom began to become bored a little watching from the shadows. Was he becoming nervous? The drummers had started beating on the drums catching up with the singers as they sang the opening song.

He could see Faith looking around the room a few times. Hope-filled his head that maybe she was looking for him. His thoughts of Faith were drowning out the song that the women were singing until they switched songs, and that was when he began to fiddle with his clothes. He began to feel the energy changing, and he peeked thru the door. Yemi's dancing was frantic as if she was possessed, and then he saw Faith squirming around in her chair. Was Faith trying to go under too? He felt a strong pull to go to her and help her. He was trying with all his might to fight that urge, but it was overpowering.

Something was pulling him, and he knew that it was not of his own doing. Could it be the drummers and that powerful song? That song called down *Asuo Geybi*, the excellent water deity. That powerful song was calling him and pulling him, and he felt like he was going to float straight to Faith. The drums, those damn drums, were intoxicating as he tried to fight the urge, no more like the desire to be with Faith. Freedom needed to feed on her, drink her essence. He longed to engulf her body with his tongue, to keep her safe from all danger. He was becoming aroused.

His senses became more alert as he began to feel that Faith had another living inside of her, and it was maddening because he could not remember if he had felt that presence when he was at her home. Those damn mushrooms! That presence was strong, and it was acting like it was trying to protect Faith from being taken, from being hurt. Freedom felt like he had to fight against it, but he was confused, for this experience was different for him. He had been with many women before, but Faith was so entirely different.

He could hear her scream, no cry out, no scream, but he could not help her. He wanted to help her, but he just could not. Everything was out of his control right now. His patience was running very thin. Faith needed him, and he was going to help her. Freedom fought his way thru until he got to her. He was finally with her, and nothing was ever going to change that. He moved in closer to her, but she did not recognize him. He wanted to scream into her ears that it was him. But she could not hear his voice. And even if she did hear his voice, she was not calm enough to recognize it and know that she was not alone.

He sniffed the air inhaling her aroma that was filling his nostrils. He wanted her, and there was going to be nothing that would prevent him from having her. He could feel the battle that she was going thru and he had to come to the presence inside her. He began speaking to it and telling it that he could not harm her but help her. The energy started to ease its tension on Faith. As soon as Faith began to come to herself, he moved to the veil. She appeared to be calmer, but he sensed her fright and her confusion. He needed her to be ok, and he hoped that she would catch a glimpse of him and know that he had been there.

She glanced towards him, but so did Nana. He had to move quickly, and he thought she had seen him as he had disappeared behind the door.

CHAPTER 22
SO WHAT HAPPENED

I SAT in the chair for god knows how long, waiting for those people to leave. I needed to ask Nana what had happened to me. How many times did a person have to give thanks or make their presence known to her? I was becoming impatient, waiting for them to finish smiling in her face and having small talk. Patience was not a virtue that I possessed. Yemi was now moving around the store, too, and was no longer standing beside me.

When the last person left the store, Yemi walked back over to me. "Are you ok," she asked.

"Yes, but I got questions."

"I know you do," she said. "But Nana will have to answer them for you. Be patient a little while longer."

"Patience, I have none," I retorted.

"You may not have patience, but you have an extraordinary gift."

What did she mean by that?

At that time, Nana walked up to us and took me by the hand. She helped me up and led me to her office, and told me to take a seat on the floor in front of her desk. I

THE DESTRUCTION OF FAITH

glanced around the room and noticed that she had many wooden statues sitting all around her office. There were pictures of her standing beside people dressed in all white or African attire. From the looks of everything, the images seemed to reveal that she must have done a lot of travel to Africa.

Yemi entered the room and immediately and took a seat beside me. She handed me a wooden cup filled with a hot liquid. "Here, sip on this to restore your energy."

I've been sitting on that gray chair for hours, and now you want to boost up my energy?

I took the cup. "Thank you." I placed my lips on the cup and began to take slow sips. The liquid was scalding, and it did not taste like any tea that I had ever drunk before. It was sweet and sour at the same time. I blew into the cup to cool it down and took a few more sips than placing the cup on the floor beside me; I said, "Now, can you please explain to me what happened to me?"

"The festival that you attended is something that we do every forty days. We must do it every forty days to maintain that bond with our ancestors," Nana answered.

"I know that part, but what happened to me," I said. I wanted to know, and I hoped that Nana sensed my agitation.

"We, the African American's in this country, have been given the duty to uphold the customs and the rituals of the Akan people who are from Ghana. The ancestors from the motherland gave *us* those permissions. The Akan people have strong connections with the *Nana Nyame*. They laid before us the foundation in which we need to stand on and rules of life that we need to live by to survive on Earth."

I picked up my cup of tea and took another sip.

She continued. "We honor the water spirits known as the *Abasoms,* and sometimes during the festival, especially during the drumming portion, a person may get possessed by the

Abasoms. That is what happened to you. You became possessed by a water spirit. "

That sounded crazy to me, but it made sense because it did feel like another presence had been inside of me other than Bella. "So, what happened to me when I became possessed?"

"Your soul or *kra* allowed it to come in and take you over," Nana responded.

I did not believe that because it felt like they had been fighting inside of me.

"When you got possessed, the water spirit calmed you down," Yemi said. I could hear so much excitement in her voice.

"What does that mean?" I asked.

"It means," Nana said, taking over the conversation. "That you needed to be a priestess or a Nana of the spirit that took you over. Nana means Priestess. While it had you, we asked for it to reveal its name, but it would not tell us what his name was."

"Him? A male spirit took me over?" I looked at both, waiting for either one to answer.

"We do not know yet, but we know that we will have to continue exploring your possibilities. I need you to start attending some of the classes. The spirits are calling you, and I want to initiate you as soon as possible."

That was still just too overwhelming. "Can you please explain to me why when I came to, you were on your knees before me handing me your beads?"

Nana seemed to become extremely uncomfortable when I asked her that question. It was like she was afraid to tell me, or maybe I was sensing something more. I knew that she was not going to give me an answer to that question. I began to feel a tingling sensation on the back of my neck, and I knew that Bella was still here. Nana was hiding something, but she never answered my question.

"Let me think on it," I said, standing up. "I need to know more about this initiation process."

"Sure, take your time, but my class will be on Saturday, and I need to know by then." Yemi stood up beside me and smiled. "I promise you that you will not be alone. I just took my rites, and I will help you as much as I can."

I smiled back at her and left her office. As I walked back into the center, the veil was moving, and something was trying to get me to walk towards it. I wanted to run from it, but it was something about the earthen pot hidden behind it that had me very curious. I started walking towards it, and when I got close enough, I placed my hands on the veil.

"What are you doing?" I heard Baba shout out to me.

I snatched my hand back. "Nothing, I was just trying to see what was in that pot."

"Well, until you have initiated with the Akan, you must never try that again." He sounded like he was angry with me for some reason. What was his deal?

"Okay, sorry for doing something wrong," I said. I walked over to my shoes, placed them on my feet, and left the store.

As I drove home, I thought that I should have asked Yemi if she had seen Freedom.

CHAPTER 23
STACEY

STACEY HAD GOTTEN up early Sunday morning before Faith's mother. She went into the kitchen and turned on the radio to allow the Sunday morning gospel to play thru the house. Stacey was glad that to remember what Faith had told her about the Sunday morning rituals. She reached into the fridge and took out the eggs and bacon. Stacey did not eat pork, but s was willing to eat it to get back at Faith. She saw that there was some flour sitting in the side door of the fridge, and she took that out too. Stacey was going to change up the energy in this house and make pancakes. She remembered that Faith used to tell her that her mother would cook the same thing every Sunday for breakfast and make her go to church.

"What the hell are you doing in my kitchen?" Ruth sounded. She was standing in the doorway. She walked into the kitchen wearing that black dress that Faith had mentioned that she always wore and took a seat at the table.

"Something that Faith has never done for you," Stacey answered. She placed the flour back in the refrigerator. "I was going to make pancakes, but I changed my mind."

Ruth pulled out a cigarette from that beaten-up green

paper box and watched Stacey move about in her kitchen like she was a professional at cooking. Stacey had made herself at home. She usually does not allow anyone to cook in her kitchen, but this was indeed refreshing. The food that she was preparing was smelling so good, and Ruth's stomach began to rumble.

Stacey began placing the food on the table.

Ruth smiled. Stacey had made her an egg and cheese omelet with four slices of bacon. Stacey sat across from her with just the omelet on her plate.

"What do you not eat pork too?" Ruth asked as she placed a slice of bacon into her mouth and bit into it.

"Well, you know. Faith got that from me just like she slept with my man. she is always copying me." Stacey began eating her eggs. Turning her mother completely against her was going to be so easy.

Ruth shook her head. "I grew up eating pork, and I have never had any issues with my blood pressure. Just eat a slice of bacon."

Stacey took a slice of bacon from Ruth's plate and bit into it. When Ruth turns her head, Stacey spits the bacon quickly into her napkin.

Ruth hurriedly ate her food and then took her plate to the sink. "I need to hurry up finish my hair. The bus will be here soon to take me to church, and I am always the first person he picks up."

"So, about that," Stacey said. "I called the church and told them that you would no longer be needing that ride. I am going to start taking you to church on Sundays."

"Are you serious?" Ruth's eyes began to water from the gesture as a tear ran down her cheek. She began sniffling.

"Why are you crying?" Stacey asked, moving towards her. She placed her arms around Ruth's shoulders.

"I have been riding that bus forever, and for you to come

in here and cook me breakfast and take me to church, well, this is the nicest thing anyone has ever done for me." Ruth began sobbing into her shoulder.

"I cannot believe that Faith has been this ungrateful child. She had me thinking that you were just mean to her. You are a great mother, and Faith just doesn't appreciate all that you do for her."

"I know," agreed Ruth. " And no matter how hard I have tried to bring her up the right way, she has always been bad, just bad." Ruth moved away from Stacey's embrace and wiped her face with her hands. She kissed her on the cheek and walked away.

Stacey watched how she walked down the hall. She almost began to feel sympathy for Ruth. Stacey believed everything Faith had told her in confidence, but she had a role to play, and all emotions could not show.

"Wow, I did not know that this was going to be this easy. Dumb bitch," she thought to herself. She cleaned up the kitchen and got ready for church.

CHAPTER 24
FAITH

I WAS BEGINNING to feel like something was not quite right. My right eye was jumping, and I sat on my pillows, trying to understand what I was feeling. I was so surprised that my mama had not called me at all yesterday. Maybe I was missing her presence some. It will take a while for me to realize that I am not living with her anymore. But something just did not feel right. I heard a knock at the door, and I went to answer it. Damn, it was that bitch Stacey. I opened the door.

"What the hell do you want?" I asked with anger.

"I want to talk to you; no, I need to talk to you," Stacey said. "Can I please come in?"

"No, for whatever you needed to say, you said it all at the club." I tried to close the door on her, but she stuck her foot out and pushed it back open.

"Please, Faith, just lend me your ears for a few minutes." She sounded like she was pleading with me.

My heart began to soften a little. I stepped aside and opened the door so that Stacey could enter. "Hurry up, and you got five minutes which is still too long for me to sit here and hear what you have to say."

Stacey moved past me, removed her shoes, and went and sat down on the pillow on the floor. "I miss you so bad," Stacey said.

"Well, I do not miss you. Please speak your mind." I closed the door behind us.

"Faith, we have been thru a lot together. I have shared so much of my life with you, and you have shared so much with me. Why can we not just chalk this up as a small misunderstanding and get past this? I want my friend back, damn it!"

I sat down beside her on the pillow. "We can never be friends again. At least not like we were. You hurt me, and I treated you like the sister that I had never had."

Stacey hung her head down. "I know, and that is why I am here to show you that I can be that friend again that you deserve to hang out with." Stacy's eyes watered.

I looked at Stacey as she sat there beside me with tears in her eyes. She was serious. I began to feel that tingling in my neck, knowing that Bella was warning me about something. Since I left the bookstore, I had not felt that tingling, and I thought that maybe she had subsided.

Stacey placed her hand on my thigh. "I want to taste you one more time. Girl, you know that the only way I can get turned on with Marcus is by thinking about you." Stacey was trying to change the energy, and it worked.

"Stop lying," I laughed. "Marcus is fine as hell, and if it were me, I would not be thinking about any other person."

"*So, she does like Marcus,*" Stacey thought to herself.

"You like him?"

"Hell no, I'm just saying that he looks good. So don't be thinking that I want your man. He is not my type. I do apologize for bringing him up at the club. But he does be looking at my ass".

"I am sorry for questioning you like that," Stacey said. "I know the type of guys you like. Besides, I have caught him plenty of times looking at asses. He is an ass man, and there are so many fat asses walking around here. Hell, he even caught me staring at your ass."

I laughed at that. "But you have good cause. You have had this fat ass so many times."

"Can I have it right now? "Stacey whispered.

"No, Stacey, not now. I have a lot to do, and besides, I told you that we could never be friends like that anymore."

"I know, but I also know that you are not wearing any panties under that skirt. Just lay back, open wide and let me eat it."

Now how was I supposed to say no to that?

CHAPTER 25
AKAN CULTURE

WHEN STACEY LEFT, my right eye was still twitching. I could not shake the feeling that something terrible was going to happen. I pulled out my cards to read them, but my mind was foggy, and I could not think straight. I kept thinking about what Nana had told me about the Akan, so I took out my laptop and researched the Akan religion.

It was fascinating the information that I had discovered. The Akan believed that they were the original peoples on this earth and that all religions flowed from their beliefs. They also believed strongly in the water and how it correlated with the moon. The power in which water possessed allowed them to have faith in the *Abasoms*, the water spirits. They had rich culture and guidelines to live by from the beginning of life until death.

The *Abasoms* had different names, and they described them as tiny beings with dread locks with back feet, which means that their feet pointed in the opposite direction. I kept trying to find any information on *Asuo-Geybi*, but there was hardly any information about him. The only information that I could find was how he had been introduced to the

THE DESTRUCTION OF FAITH

Akan by another tribe who honored the spirits of the dead. But, there was so much information about his daughters, and I imagined that I was his daughter. The person who wrote the article stated that he only comes to those initiated under him and only the women.

That was interesting. Being already drawn to *Asuo-Gyebi's* energy, I am ready to be initiated. I could not wait until Saturday for this spirituality class. I closed my laptop and called Nana. I asked her if I could come to the bookstore. She told me that she had been waiting on my phone call. I was beginning to believe that this woman was a mind reader and intuitive. I reopened my laptop. I was so excited, for the more I read about the Akan deities, the more I felt connected.

It was like I was from Ghana. I heard about this DNA test that you do online to trace your bloodline. I would do a DNA test from Ancestry to find out my bloodline as soon as possible. If I was from the Akan, then I knew why I was attracted to the religion. But what was so odd was that all this talk about the Akan people and their deities had me feeling like I was becoming very aroused.

When I arrived at the bookstore, there were several cars parked. I hope that I can find a space. But there was one space in front of the door. It was like that space was for me. I pulled into it and parked my car. I turned off the ignition and hesitated a little before getting out of the car and walking into the store. As soon I entered the store, there stood Freedom. He was standing there grinning from ear to ear all up in another woman's face.

What the hell was he doing here?

I spoke to the other women standing around him, and he

looked at me like I needed to address him too, but I ignored him. At least I was trying to.

He was wearing an aquatic blue African-style shirt and smiling hard at one of the women, almost wearing the same style shirt. Nana was standing near the counter speaking with Baba. She spotted me and motioned me towards the center. I could not believe that Freedom had not spoken to me. What kind of game was he playing, and why was he with that girl? Well, at least it looked like he was with that sister.

Okay, I needed to calm down before I woke her up. I was kind of jealous to see Freedom standing there chatting it up with this lady. I thought at least he would have been happy to see me when I entered the bookstore, but he was too busy being happy for someone else. Well, it is his loss. But I must remind myself that he did tell me that he was not looking for someone to chill with at the time. I need to focus on what is going on with my spiritual life.

I took off my shoes and sat down. I pulled out my phone and began browsing thru it.

"Hi Faith, how have you been?" I looked up from my phone, and it was Freedom, and he was grinning from ear to ear like a Cheshire cat. I put my head down, ignoring him, still searching thru my phone.

He took the phone out of my hands. "I asked you a question."

"I have been doing okay, and you?" I wanted to curse Freedom out, but my stupid ass just did as he asked and succumbed to his energy.

"I am okay. I heard that you were here the other day," he responded.

So, my mind had been playing tricks on me. Freedom had not been there.

"I was," I stated.

THE DESTRUCTION OF FAITH

"I am happy that you are here today. I was hoping that I would see you again," Freedom replied.

He was staring at me like I was supposed just to grin and be all gushy on the inside because he was hoping that he would have been able to see me. Give me a fucking break. I just stared at him, looking all silly, smiling at me.

"Is that right?"

"That sounds like you do not believe me," he said.

"If you say so, but please give me back my phone." He handed it to me.

Just as I was about to tell him how I felt, Nana walked into the center. I glanced up at her, and I could have sworn that I saw a glimpse of jealousy in her eyes. I blinked my eyes and glanced back at her. Maybe I was wrong because now she was all smiling and very friendly. She was acting too sweet.

She sashayed over to us. "You know, Freedom; you have a lot to do before you leave, so why are you over here messing with my next initiate?"

Freedom stood up and looked at her sternly. I could have sworn that as I watched his expression, it was one of mistrust towards Nana. My head began tingling.

"I did not know that you were going to initiate," he said to me, never taking his eyes off me. It was more like a statement versus a question.

Nana smiled. "Of course, she is." Nana rubbed my arm. "I need her to be part of my shrine. She has an incredible gift, and I am going to be the one to harvest that for her."

"Harvest?" Freedom said. "What is there for you to harvest? It's her gift." He spoke like he had authority over her. What the hell was going on here?

"Did I say harvest, no I meant to say shape," Nana said, retracting her use age of the word.

I cleared my throat to get the attention back on me. The back of my head was beginning to throb even more now, and something was not quite right between them. Whatever it was, Bella did not want me around him. I guess she did not leave me after all.

"I just stopped by to ask you a question, and I didn't mean for the two of you to be discussing me like this. Hell, I was not even expecting you to be here." I looked at Freedom.

"One thing you will learn when you become a part of my shrine is that I do not tolerate any type of curse words spoken in my presence. Therefore, coming to classes is a must because it helps you to understand the proper protocol when you are in the presence of your elders."

I felt like I was being scolded again by my mama but in a more dignified way.

"Look, I am just gonna go," I said. "Maybe we can do this another time." I stood up.

Freedom spoke. "No, do not leave. I am the one who has intruded on your space. I will visit you another time."

Before I could protest, he walked out of the room, and maybe he glided because it was so smooth, and it felt like a cool breeze kissed me on my cheek. It felt like the cool breeze that envelops you when standing on the sands at the beach. I watched him leave the room.

"Now, what is it that you want to talk to me about?" Nana asked.

"I have not been doing so well," I replied.

"What is wrong with you?" she asked. She seemed genuinely concerned.

"I do not know. It's not that I have not been feeling well, but I have not seen my mother, and she has not reached out to me in a couple of days."

"So, I gather that you and your mother do not have a great relationship?"

"No, we don't. My mother is a very abusive woman and a pathological liar," I said.

THE DESTRUCTION OF FAITH

Nana's facial expression became stern. "We are not supposed to speak of our mother that way." Immediately I felt ashamed as if once again I was being scolded for telling the truth. "You may be right, but you do not understand the things that I have been thru in my life. Nevertheless, that is not why I am here." I needed to change the subject because I was not too fond of it when people took up for her, and no one recognized the scars that I wear on my back which were so heavy to carry.

I watched this movie, *Beloved*, starring Oprah Winfrey. During the film, Oprah's character is beaten by a whip repeatedly striking across her back. Once the wounds healed, they caused a tree to form there. Throughout the movie, she spoke of a tree being on her back. It was a heavy load to carry when all you knew was pain and torment, and you could not escape your tormentor. Whenever someone attempted to take up for my mother, the pain and misery that I suffered would resurface. Oprah never did outrun hers either because it came in the form of her dead daughter that she had killed.

Maybe my mother was Oprah, and I was the dead daughter, her tormentor. Did my mother view me as a heavy scar from her past? Did she think that I was a burden that she had to carry? I need to get out of my head. I focused my attention back on Nana.

"I feel like I am part of the Akan. I cannot explain it, but I feel *Asuo-Geybi* has touched me in the inside part, and I want to know more about him. I want to initiate as soon as possible." I felt a sharp twinge in the back of my neck, and I grabbed my neck.

"Are you ok?" she asked.

"No, I keep having these sensations in the back of my neck." I began to massage the back of my neck slowly.

"Sit down, Faith," she said to me.

I sat down.

"Spirit enters your body from the back of your neck. When the spirit leaves, it also leaves a piece of itself with you, and you may be experiencing the residue from the festival."

"No, this has been with me as long as I can remember. It started when I was twelve, and it continued. Especially when I feel nervous or threatened."

Nana was staring at me, and she had a smirk on her face. She knew something but was not telling me. Nana knew what was going on with me, and I began to sense that Freedom was right. She wanted to take my gift, but the word she used was harvest. The pain was starting to become more intensified, and I stood up. My phone fell to the floor, and I reached down to pick it up.

As I stood up, I saw what looked like Freedom standing behind the veil. Was he eavesdropping on us?

"I need for you to be here on Friday morning before the sun rises. We will begin the rite then."

"So soon?" I was squinching from the pain in my neck.

"Yes, the sooner, the better," she said as she stood up.

"We need to help you be able to control your gift, so this needs to happen right away."

"Ok," I said. "I will be here."

As I started to walk out the way I had come in through the store, she stopped me.

"Please use the side entrance. The store is pretty crowded today, and I do not want you to absorb others' negative energy when you move past them."

That did make sense because I was going to initiate, and I needed to make sure that nothing would attach to me. Nana guided me out the back of the entrance. I walked around to the side of the store towards my car. I glanced over in the parking lot, and I noticed a vehicle there which looked familiar. But the pain in my head was starting to be enormous, and I got straight in my car and drove home.

Nana sat in the gray chair after Faith had left and looked at the veil. She saw movement but did not see Freedom. Nana knew why Freedom was here, but it was difficult to control him, and Nana knew it would be difficult because he liked Faith. She closed her eyes and meditated.

CHAPTER 26
MAMA

As I was driving home, I decided to go past my mother's house to see if she was sitting on the porch. I did not see her when I drove past the house, and the front door was closed. She usually sits on the front porch with the front door is open. Even if she sits in the backyard, she still leaves the front door open with the screen door locked.

I made a U-turn in the middle of the street and pulled up in front of the house. I got out of the car and walked up the hill to the house. My mother's house sat on top of a steep hill. It was always a pain walking up that hill. I always ran out of breath, but I was not out of breath this time as I walked up the driveway. I needed to see what was going on with her.

I tried to open the screen door, but it would not budge, that was odd, but it also meant that she was in the house. I knocked a few times on the screen door, but no answer,

"Mama!" I shouted. I peeped thru the window, and I could see the television was playing, but she was not sitting there on the couch watching it.

"What the hell is going on?" I thought to myself.

I walked to the back of the house, and the back door was

THE DESTRUCTION OF FAITH

open. I pulled on the screen door, but it gave way. I walked into the house.

"Mama!" I yelled out again.

No answer.

"*Is she asleep?*" I asked myself.

I started walking down the hallway towards her room, and I heard strange sounds coming from my old bedroom. Something was not feeling right, and the pain was beginning to pierce the back of my head.

"Ma, where you at," I called out.

The noises that I heard were louder. I needed to see what was happening in my room. As I moved closer to the door, I heard a strange noise coming from the bathroom, and I smelled a familiar scent. It smelled like Egyptian Musk, the oil that Stacey is always wearing. It smelled like it was coming from my old room. I placed my hand on the doorknob to open the door to see if she was in my room.

"What the hell are you doing?" Mama said, walking out of the bathroom.

I jerked my hand away; she had startled me. "I came by to check on you, mama. How are you?"

Mama stood there with a big yellow towel wrapped around her body.

"I am good. Now leave."

"Mama, please let us not do this. I wanted to see how you were doing, but I guess you are okay. But do you have time to chat? I need to talk about what is happening to me. I need to tell you what I am planning on doing."

Mama walked down the hallway past me and went into her room. I stood outside her door, waiting on her to get dressed and come out. I was never allowed to go inside her room, and I stood there like a little girl waiting on permission for her to invite me in. I knew that would not happen, so I stood there waiting for her to come out. She had slipped on that old house dress that she loves to wear and walked right past me.

I followed her as we went into the living room.

"I already know what you been up to," she said.

I waited for her to pull out a Salem, but she did not pick up the cigarettes. "You are trying to quit after all these years?" I asked.

"No, just taking a break. But as I said, I know what you have done. I never thought the day would come that my daughter would be a fucking whore! You should be ashamed of yourself. I know all about your little ass," she snapped.

"You know what, mom; I think that I am going to leave. I have no idea what you are referring to, but I just wanted to tell you that I am going to get a DNA test with Ancestry to see where we are from."

"What are you doing that for?" I sensed anxiety coming from my mother.

"Because I am on a new journey in my life, and I need some answers."

My mother's mood changed, and she became quiet. "What will that show?"

Why was she starting to want to talk to me?

"I cannot believe that you want to be interested in what I want to do. Just a few seconds ago, you called me names, and now you want to ask about my DNA test?

Then she became the mother that I knew and hated. "Fuck you bitch! I do not give a damn about that. I want you out of my house right now!" She was yelling at me and shouting at me with insults and telling me that I was whore. It was the same rhetoric repeatedly; I was very ungrateful for what people had done for me. The pain was sharper than ever at the back of my neck. It was like it had graduated from just being a tingling sensation, and I had this overwhelming

THE DESTRUCTION OF FAITH

feeling to grab her by her tiny throat and choke the hell out of her.

I started walking towards the kitchen instead. I would not stand here and allow Mama to keep insulting me and calling me out of my name.

"Yeah, you better run!" she screamed at me as I walked out of her house.

CHAPTER 27
RUTH

RUTH WENT BACK to her room and began taking off the house dress. She could not believe that Faith had the nerve to come to her house and act like she was all that. *If I needed her, I would call her, but who does she think she is,* she thought to herself.

Ruth had been taking her a long hot bath and thinking about how nice it was to have Stacey living there. Stacey was friendly and had been so considerate by taking her to church. It was a good feeling riding in a car for a change instead of being on that bus every Sunday.

Hell, Faith had a car now, and she still had not asked to give her a ride to church. Her daughter was so ungrateful. But Stacey had been a welcoming change for her. Stacey had come in her house doing more for her than Faith had ever done. All Faith could do was bring her pain and shame. Shame it will bring into her life if she finds out her father's identity.

Now she wants to go and get a DNA test to see where her family resided. Ruth was overly concerned about that. She did not want her to find out who her father was. As Ruth slipped on her sundress, there was a knock at the door. *"This better not*

THE DESTRUCTION OF FAITH

be Faith coming back here," she thought to herself. Because if it was, she was going slap her dead in her face.

Knock, Knock. Knock.

"I'm coming!" she said, yelling at the top of her lungs. Ruth snatched the door open, and it was her stepfather standing there.

"What you want, you never come here," she snarled at him. She gave him a disgusted look.

He ignored that look that he was used to receiving from her. "I know, but I wanted to tell you something. Is my granddaughter here?"

Ruth pushed past him, almost hitting him with the screen door as she stepped out on the porch. "Nope, she moved out."

"Oh, I see. I wanted to talk to both of you."

"About what?" she asks.

"I got some bad news a few months ago, and I wanted to let you two know what was going on with me," her stepfather said with sadness.

"Look, David," Ruth said. "We do not need you coming around here right now." She sat down in her favorite rocking chair and slowly began to rock. The chair was squeaking with every movement as if it were tired of her too.

"I know that it has been a while, but I do want to tell you something." David sat down in one of the rocking chairs opposite Ruth.

"Spit it out," she sounded.

"Last month, I got diagnosed with pancreatic cancer, and I wanted to let you two know that I do not have that much time left."

"Get the fuck out of here!" Ruth exclaimed. She stopped rocking.

"Yes, it's true. I know that I have not been around much, and I know that you hate me for not being a grandfather to her as to my other grandchildren, but I want to make things right," Davide pleaded.

Ruth laughed. "You want to make things right. That is so funny, man. I went thru a lot, and I had no family to turn to help me. You even turned my mother against me before she died. Now because you got cancer, you want to come around here to make amends. Get the fuck out of here!"

David stood up. He knew that it was going to be difficult trying to speak to them after all these years. If Faith had been there, she would have made it better for him, and that would have been a welcoming distraction from Ruth. Even though he hardly came around them, Faith would still be highly excited to see him whenever he did show his face. He knew that he should have done better by them. "Ruth, I know you are upset with me, but I need to make my peace before I leave this world."

Ruth looked up at him. she reached into the ashtray, removed a half-smoked cigarette, and lit it. She inhaled then blew the smoke straight up in his face.

"You know you are still crazy as hell," David said, wiping the smoke away from his face.

"Yep, now get the fuck off my porch!" she exclaimed.

David began moving towards the steps. He stopped walking and turned around to face her. "Please tell Faith that I came by when you see her, and please tell her what I said."

"Hell naw, you call that little bitch yourself!"

David could not believe that she had called her daughter a bitch. "What is wrong with you?" he asked.

"Nothing, I am sick of her, and I'm sick of you too. I need the two of you to leave me the fuck alone."

"I have you left you alone for years. But right now, I am trying to apologize for not being the father that you needed in your life. Can you at least give me her number so that I may call her?" David grabbed his side as a sharp pain hit him.

"Hell, naw fucker!" Ruth snarled. Ruth saw the grimace on his face from the pain. She began to calm down a little; after all, he was dying. "She just left turning up on Southgate Drive. If you hurry, you may catch her at the light."

David quickly walked off the porch and went to his car. Hopefully, he could catch her to tell her what was going on with him. He knew that she would not talk to him like Ruth had done. Faith would be gentler to him.

CHAPTER 28
FAITH AND DAVID

I WAS SITTING at the stoplight at Burger King when I heard a car horn blaring crazily at me. I glanced over to my left, and it was my grandfather. A huge smile came across my face. I motioned for him to follow me. When the light turned green, he followed me into Food Lion's parking lot. Before he could turn the ignition off on his car, I jumped out of my car and ran over to his car.

"Hurry up and get out!" I exclaimed.

My grandfather got out of the car and gave me a big hug.

"What are you doing in Raleigh?" I asked.

"I came to visit you and your mother," David said, hugging her tightly. "She told me that you had moved."

I stepped back from him. "I did move. I have my place over near Cameron village."

"You look well, " he said, grinning.

"Thank you," I chimed.

"I need to talk to you about something, and I do not have that much time. May I get in your car?" he looked sad.

"Sure" I went to my car and opened the door for him. I had not seen him in years, and it was a pleasure to see my

THE DESTRUCTION OF FAITH

grandfather. He was always so kind to me, and he never allowed my mother to be mean to me whenever he was around.

I climbed into the car on the driver's side. "So, what's up?" I asked.

"Well, I am not going to be here long," he said.

"What you mean by that," I quizzed,

"I have cancer, and it's a four-stage level now. I tried to talk to your mama, but all she did was curse at me."

"Wait, what? You have what?" I was still stuck on the cancer part.

"Yes, the doctor told me that I have not long to live, so I wanted to come by and tell you and Ruth this."

I did not know how to take what he was saying to me. We hardly ever went around them, but when we did, all hell would break loose. Mama would say some negative mess, and then we were either kicked out of the house or told to leave. But my grandfather would pull me to the side and tell me that he loved me and that if I ever needed him to call him. I would hide his telephone number or try to remember it before Mama would find it and rip it up.

I always wanted to spend more time with him because even though he was not my real grandfather and he could be firm with me at times, whenever we were together, he still would tell me that he loved me. Something that my mother never did. Now he was telling me that he was dying, and this was driving me crazy. I needed more time to spend with him, to get to know him more. To show him my place and just let him know that I was not my mother. Now I was an adult, and she no longer had a rule over me.

"I am sorry to hear that, but I know that no matter what, things will be okay."

He grabbed my hand, "They will."

A thought popped in my head. "Why don't you come to my house tonight for dinner? Are you staying in Raleigh?"

"Well, I wanted to drive back home, but I think that I will stay the night."

I was so happy because we would talk freely without mama's eyes spying on us with her negativity. I wrote my address down on a piece of paper lying on the floor of my car and handed it to him.

"What time do we eat?" he asked.

"Come over around five. I try to eat my meals before six. I need to watch my weight," I laughed. "Oh, and do not worry about sleeping in a hotel. You can stay at my house!"

He reached over and kissed me on the cheek. "I cannot wait."

CHAPTER 29
STACEY

STACEY WALKED into the house and saw Ruth sprawled out the couch. *She is such a slob,* she thought to herself. *I can see why Faith hated her.* All she did was sit on the porch and smoke cigarettes and weed all day. She had no idea how she managed to keep the rent paid and the lights on.

Ruth had told her that she had lost her license, and she received a disability check which brought the money in. She probably lied about that just to sit on her ass all day and not do shit. Ruth was not an ugly woman, but her personality made her that way. She was small frame and had an ample derriere. Faith used to tell her how she wished that she was shaped like her mother all the time.

Stacey could not believe that Faith had not run away years ago. This woman was unbearable, but Stacey had managed to put on her game face to get her revenge against Faith. Ruth began stirring on the couch.

"Ruth, I'm home," Stacey sang.

Ruth opened her eyes and sat up on the couch. "I'm sorry, baby, I did not know you were here." She rubbed the sleep out of her eyes.

"I just walked in the house," Stacey replied.

"You know who came over here today?" Ruth asked.

"Faith?"

"Yes, who else. Faith acted like she was about to go into your room, and I stopped that."

"What did she want?" Stacey asked.

"She was just checking on me. She thinks that she is so much better than me," Ruth answered. She reached over into the glass ashtray sitting on the table and removed a half-smoked blunt.

"She acts like that with everybody, and I hope that I never see her again because I promise you, Miss Ruth, It will not be nice."

Ruth noticed that Stacey was holding two paper bags. It looked like Chinese food. "What you got there?" Ruth asked her. She was nosey.

"I stopped by that Chinese place near the arena and got us some food for dinner. You do like Chinese food, don't you?"

"Girl, I love it, especially shrimp fried rice."

"Well, sit back down, and I will bring your plate to you."

Ruth sat down, and Stacey took the food into the kitchen. She took two plates down from the cupboard and removed the small white cartons from the paper bag. The carton contained the shrimp fried rice; Stacey added some of that to one of the plates. Stacey glanced around to ensure that Ruth was not watching her as she removed a small vial from her purse. It contained white powder and sprinkled it on the food. She then fixed her plate and went back into the living room. She handed Ruth her plate.

"I have not had this in a long time, "Ruth said. She was happy that someone was concerned about her well-being.

"It's not a big matter. I live here too, and when I stop to get something to eat, you can have something too." Stacey ate

THE DESTRUCTION OF FAITH

her food slowly as she watched Ruth stuff the rice and shrimp down her throat as she had never eaten food like this before. She was waiting for her to ingest the food to start asking her questions about Faith.

When she had purchased the vial, it guaranteed that the stuff would make people speak the truth. Whatever secrets hide inside a person would come out, and she planned on finding out all of Ruth's secrets.

CHAPTER 30
FAITH

When I pulled up in front of my house Freedom was sitting on my porch. *He got some nerve being here. What the hell did he want?* I walked up to the steps and moved right past him. I unlocked the door and went inside, shutting the door behind me and locking it. I heard him knocking at the door, and I waited for a few minutes before opening the door.

"Why are you playing?" " he smiled at me.

"Why are you here uninvited? Go back to where you come from."

"I can't do that right now. I am here for you now," Freedom said.

"Oh, really, and who else? I saw you smiling at those groupies today at the store."

"Do I sense some jealousy," he teased.

"Nope, not all," I retorted. But deep down inside, I was a little jealous. "What can I do you for?"

"I wanted to talk to you about the initiation that you are going to do," Freedom said.

"Why? That is none of your business," I retorted.

THE DESTRUCTION OF FAITH

"I know that it isn't, but do you know what you are about to do?" he asked. Freedom was concerned about her.

I shook my head. "Nope, but I do know that I need it. You were not there when I got possessed, and I want to know more about the Akan and the water spirits. I want to know more about their culture. I will do my DNA kit tonight and mail it off tomorrow to determine if my ancestors were from Ghana. I need to know where I came from."

"You do not have to initiate to find that out. You have an incredible gift, and you do not need to have anyone over you trying to control it and stop you from being who you are supposed to be." Freedom said with much earnestness in his voice, but I also heard a little sternness there.

I looked at him. "How do you know what type of gift I have?"

"I know that you possess something deep inside of you. I know that you have no clue what it is about, and I know that it empowers you."

Freedom knew so much, and this was crazy because how did he know all this. "That might be true, but I am drawn to *Asuo-Gyebi*. Whenever I hear his name and say it, I feel like he is calling me to him and has placed a calling on my life. I just want to be one of his priestesses."

"What do you know about *Asuo-Gyebi?*" he asked. "Why do you want to be a priestess of his and share him with all his other priestesses?"

"Nothing except what I read from the information that Nana gave me," I answered. "I feel that it means something to belong to him, and I just want to belong." I hung my head down.

"Hmm," he said, placing his hands together. He leaned back against the wall. "Let me tell you the truth about him. *Asuo-Gyebi* is not a Abasom. He is a deified Ancestor. He was brought over to the Americas some 300 years ago, and people have turned him into a god or Abasom of the Akan folk. He belongs to the Guan people."

"So, you telling me that he did not possess me? Nan told me that he took me over." I hope that Nana was not lying to me because I needed to trust her, and I needed to have something substantial to believe in to help me understand what was going on with me spiritually.

"They have no idea which spirit possessed you. They were trying to get you to tell them what his name was."

"How do you know that if you were not there?" He was not even there, so how does he know what happened?

"Yemi told me all about it," he said as if it was no big deal that someone was telling my business. I wonder how many more people did she speak to about my business?

As if he could read my mind, he spoke. "Yemi is my best friend too, and she knows that I have an interest in you."

So, he finally admitted it to me. He does like me.

"No, interested," he replied.

"Get out of my head," I said.

Freedom stared at me with an expressionless face. "I am never getting out of your head until you are safe," he said. "I came here to protect you. You do not know how powerfully you can become, and you do not have to initiate.."

I reached over to the bowl sitting on the floor beside the small table that I had placed against the wall and pulled out my small glass pipe. I took the herb from there and put some into the tube. I lit it and pulled on it.

"Why do you do so many drugs?" he said to me as if he was not approving of my lifestyle.

"I do whatever I want to do," I snapped. "I have been thru so much in life, and it helps me to think. Why are you coming at me?"

"Hold on, Faith, I'm not coming at you. I am just asking you a question. I meant no harm."

THE DESTRUCTION OF FAITH

He was right. He probably didn't mean any harm, but I am always keeping my guard up. It becomes difficult to allow anyone to come in and be a part of your circle. Shit, I just found out that my best friend is two-faced. Then right when I feel like I can be a part of something, I am being told that I was lied to again. Will it ever stop?

I put the pipe down and pulled my cell phone out of my bag. I needed to get up and start cooking dinner for my grandfather. I had almost forgotten that he was coming over for dinner.

"Freedom, if you do not have any plans, would you like to stay and have dinner with me? My grandfather is on his way over here, and I would like for you to know him and meet him." I was changing the subject to avoid his question and the whole conversation altogether. To answer his question would mean that I would have to bring up bad memories and reveal my ugly truths. I did not want to talk about my mother, who had driven me to this.

"I thought that it was just you and your mother?" he asked. He removed his shoes and placed them by the door.

"Well, it has been just she and I for a long time because she always manages to cut us off from the family. Are you staying?"

"I took off my shoes, didn't I," he laughed. He walked over to me and helped me off the floor. We walked into the kitchen, and I started rummaging thru the fridge, trying to find something to cook for us. I know that he had cancer, but I had no idea what he was allowed to eat. I had some veggie burger meat, and I pulled that and placed it on the counter. Freedom reached over into my vegetable basket and removed onion and a clove of garlic. He took the drawer from the drawer and cut them up into small pieces using the cutting board. I said nothing as he tossed the vegetables in with the meat, and I began to stir it all together.

He walked over to the fridge and took out a bag of frozen white corn. I had a green pepper in the refrigerator, and he took that out, cut it up with more onions, and added it to the corn. I smiled at him, and he smiled back. *I did not know that he was a cook.* I reached up into my cabinet and took out a box of green matcha tea with some peppermint tea as well. I removed eight bags, four of each, and placed them into a quart-size pot. He smiled at me, and I smiled back. It was strange how we smiled at each other and how we just moved in sync in my kitchen. I could get used to this, but who knows. We finished preparing the meal, and I set the table for three as I waited for my grandfather's arrival.

Freedom had walked into the living room and had plugged his cell phone into my blue tooth speaker. I began to hear a song by *Howling Wolf* vibrating against the speaker and bouncing off my walls.

"I didn't know that you liked the blues?" I asked. I was glad because music hardly ever got played in my mom's house. I fell in love with blues music by watching *Crossroads'* years ago.

"Yes, I love this music." Freedom was smiling so hard and began moving around and shuffling like he was dancing to the blues. I joined him, and he spun me around singing in my ear. I was laughing so hard because he could not sing, and it was so funny to me when he began to howl like a wolf.

"Boy, you are so stupid," I giggled.

He howled back at me.

Suddenly we heard a loud knock at the front door. I moved away from Freedom and went to open the door.

"It must be my grandfather," I spoke. I picked up a small bottle of air fresher sitting on my table and began spraying it in the air.

"Do you want me to light an incense?"

THE DESTRUCTION OF FAITH

"Yes, please. I do not want my grandfather to know that I smoke weed."

"Hmm, what happened to me? I can do whatever I want to do," he teased.

"I can but out of respect, and I do not want him to know. We must respect our elders, as Nana would say."

When I swung the door open, it was my mother standing there with Stacey. What the fuck?

CHAPTER 31
MOM AND STACEY

"What the hell are you two doing here!" I exclaimed. I was not expecting to see them at my door. I thought that it was my grandfather. My mother moved past Stacey and walked into my house like it was her house. I was beginning to get pissed off, and I felt that tingling on the back of my neck.

Slow down, Bella.

"Sorry to bother you," Stacey said, looking at a Freedom when she entered. "But your mom called me and asked me to bring her to see you. She said that she had to tell you something important."

Freedom went to his phone and unplugged it, turning off the music.

I was in such a good mood, and here she comes once again, trying to spoil everything for me. "Ma, what do you want?"

"Well, you didn't tell me where you stayed, and I wanted to see your place." My mother walked around my living room, turning her nose up at how it looked and treating my sacred space like it was filthy.

THE DESTRUCTION OF FAITH

"I thought I taught you better than this. Why do you get pillows on the floor instead of furniture?" She leaned up against the wall.

"Mama, this is my house, and I fix it up the way I see fit." Freedom moved closer to me, for he felt my whole mood change.

"And who is this fine young man," she said, smiling hard at him.

I was beginning to feel angry, and I did not want Freedom to see that side of me, so I tried to calm *Bella* down. "Mama, this is my friend Freedom. Freedom Ruth."

Freedom smiled and leaned over to her, and kissed her on the cheek. "It is a pleasure to finally meet the woman that gave birth to such a beautiful person as your daughter."

He was laying it on too thick.

I watched Stacey roll her eyes at him as she was disgusted. I made a facial expression at her to behave.

"How do you do," Ma said in her sweetest tone.

"Why did it sound like she was flirting with him?" I thought to myself.

"I can see where she gets her beauty. You and Faith look so much alike," he said, backing away from her.

"Well, the difference between Faith and me is that I am a real woman, and she is trying to be one. Besides, she is way fatter than me," responded Mama.

I wanted to slap the shit out of her for speaking on me like that. But I needed to stay calm so that nothing would erupt. "Ma, what do you want? " I wanted her to hurry up and leave before grandaddy arrived.

"Well, I came to tell you that David, I mean your grandfather dropped by to see me today," she answered.

"Ma, I know I saw him at the grocery store. He is on his way over here now to have dinner with me."

Ruth stood up straight and glared at me. "I do not want you spending no time alone with him. You should have told me that you had invited him here!"

"Ma, this is my house, and I am very much a grown woman. I do not need your permission to invite anyone to my home." I could feel the tension elevating, and I had no desire to stop it.

"You need to call him right now and tell him that I am here, and he needs not to come over here and bother you!" My mother was screaming in my ear and had gotten all in my face. She spoke to me like I was a little girl in front of Freedom, and I was so embarrassed.

"I am not telling him anything," I spoke as calmly as I could, but she needed to get out of my face.

Mama was beginning to act furious, and she was pushing it to the limit. Stacey moved in between us because my mother worked like she was about to strike me, and I would not back down in my home. I could feel the tingling in the back of my neck becoming fiercer, and I knew that I would let her out.

I was not caring about who was around us. I closed my eyes because I felt the release, then Freedom grabbed me and pulled me into the kitchen. I opened my eyes. It was as if he knew what was about to happen, and he was preventing it.

"Faith, please do not allow your mother to get you upset," he said to me in a hushed tone. "Let it go and shake it off."

I shook my head at him in aggravation. "See, this is the reason why I do not speak of her. She has been treating me like this my whole life."

"I know she has. It seemed like the special people go thru so much hell," he said to me. "Well, your grandfather is on his way, so I will politely ask her to leave." He started to walk into the living room, but he stopped and turned back to look

THE DESTRUCTION OF FAITH

at me. "I know that you are upset and everything, but just calm down. I can see you have a fire in your eyes, and I do not want you to hit your mother."

I glared at him. I knew that he was not taking my mother's side, but it felt like he was trying to protect her from me. Stacey walked into the kitchen and stood behind me while Freedom was talking to me. She was standing so close to me that I could feel her breasts touching my back.

I turned around to face her. "Why did you bring her here without calling me to see if it would be okay for her to come?" I yelled at her. I wanted to hit her too.

"I wanted to surprise you. Miss Ruth told me that all she wanted to do was make a truce with you and wanted to see your house," she answered. After they had finished eating their Chinese food, Stacey had encouraged Ruth to visit Faith. Ruth had jumped on the idea, for she also wanted to see if Faith and David were together. Stacey knew that Faith would fly off the handle if she saw her mother.

Stacey was lying to me, and I could feel it. "But you could have called first. I have company, and soon another guest will appear. I want you to take her home."

Stacey cut her eyes at Freedom. "So, is this your new boo?"

"No, we are just friends, but what if it was? It's none of your business." I replied.

Stacey acted like she was about to respond to what I had just said when my mother stormed in. "Stacey, take me home. This ungrateful bitch does not want me here, and I do not want to be here!"

I moved towards her, and Freedom touched me. I pushed his hand away from me. "The more I think that things will become better with us, the more you show me that you will never change. At times I wish that I was never born to you!"

She spat on my floor, and I felt heat coming from Freedom. He was beginning to become upset, and I felt like finally, someone was taking up for me.

"Miss Ruth, please do not be disrespectful like that in your daughter's home," I heard Freedom say to her. "To spit on someone's floor in their house is to curse them!"

"Who the fuck is you?" she asked him. All the soft tones she had with him earlier flew straight out the door.

"I am someone who cares about your daughter, and that was not right of you to spit on her floor like that, disrespecting her home." Freedom stood there with sincerity written on his face, but I sense something more. He was trying to hide his anger. He looked back at me, and at that moment, I realized that he knew why I smoke weed all the time.

I could see the anger in my mother's face and also hear the anxiety in her voice. I knew that she was about to lash out at him. "This is my fucking daughter, and I can do whatever I want to in her home! You need to stay out of my mother-fucking business and tend to your affairs. All you are going to do is fuck her and leave anyway. That is what men do. They fuck you, and they leave you!"

"C'mon, Miss Ruth, let's go," Stacey said. She had moved closer to her. She started pulling on her arm to leave when there was a knock at the door.

I was hoping that my mother had left before my grandfather got there. I did not need all this negative energy in my home. Freedom did not say a word but went to answer the door.

"Hi, is Faith Richardson here?" I heard a male voice ask. It did not sound like my grandfather. I hurriedly walked into the living room.

"Yes, that's me," I said, walking to the front door. To my

THE DESTRUCTION OF FAITH

surprise, two policemen were standing there. "How can I help you?"

"Mam' I hate to tell you this, but there has been a bad car accident," he replied. Before he got the words out of his mouth, I knew what it was. I fell to the floor.

CHAPTER 32
YOUR GRANDFATHER DIED

WHEN I CAME TO, my head was lying on the pillow on the floor. Stacey and my mother were gone, and Freedom was sitting beside me with a glass of water. "What happens?" I asked him as I tried to raise my head.

"Well, you fainted, " he said. "Here, why don't you take a sip of water." He handed me the glass of water.

I took a few sips, and it tasted lemony. "What is in this?" I asked. It did not taste bad, but it threw me off.

"It's lemon water."

I drank some more and handed him the glass.

"I am so sorry for your loss," he said to me. His voice was full of sadness.

"I do not understand." *What was he talking about, my loss?*

"Before you could hear what the officer had to say, you fainted. He was telling you that your grandfather was killed in a terrible accident by a drunk driver., When they searched the car, they found your address on a slip of paper, and that is why they came here."

Tears began streaming down my face. I could not believe that he was dead. I had just seen him hours ago, and he had

THE DESTRUCTION OF FAITH

told me that he would die from cancer. How could this be happening to me? Just when I was beginning to have joy at knowing that he and I could be family, A real family without my mother interfering, then this happened.

"He said that your grandfather was walking out of the flower shop with some sunflowers, and the driver lost control of their car and drove onto the sidewalk running him over." Freedom was trying to be gentle with his words. He did not want to keep adding on to her anguish.

Tears were flowing down my cheeks and dropping into my lap. I could not speak. I could feel pain and sorrow. I also was having regret not spending time with him. I began to cry. "Why are bad things always happening to me? Every time I think that I am finally going to find or have some piece of happiness, here comes the boom. Where did they go?" I said to him through my tears.

"Well, your mother was sobbing so hard she was acting like she was going to be sick, so Stacey took her home."

"Good, she should have never been here in the first place. She probably caused the accident by bringing that negative energy into my home."

Freedom got up and walked over to my bookcase; he pulled down a blue notebook and handed it to me. "I hope you don't mind, but I found this laying on the floor behind this pillow. I picked the notebook up and was about to place it back on the shelf."

He handed me the book, and I took it from him and opened it. It was my book of poems.

"Why are you giving this to me." I was puzzled. I wiped my tears off my face with my hands.

"I was skimming thru it, and I stumbled upon this poem that you wrote. I need you to read it." He stood there waiting for me to respond. "I want you to read the poem you wrote about family.

I flipped the pages until I saw the one that was titled *Family*. As I read the poem, I began to cry. The following few stanzas said how I wish my grandfather would bring me sunflowers one day, but he would probably get hit by a car with my bad luck. I threw the book down on the floor. "No, no, no!" I screamed. "This cannot be happening. I did not kill him!"

"No, you did not, but your poems come to life. It is like when you write about something, and it happens. Sometimes it manifests quickly, and it happens right away. If it doesn't happen right away, it soon comes true. That is the gift that I was telling you that you have. That is the gift that you possess, and others want to take it from you."

"What are you talking about!" I cried. "I did not want my grandfather to die. Forget about that gift. it killed my grandfather!" I threw the book across the room, and it hit the wall.

"No, it did not kill him; you foresaw it. You have so much power inside of you that you have yet to tap into your true self."

I stood up and looked down at him. "That is why I am going to take that initiation. I need to know how to control this so that no one else will get hurt." I began to shake.

Freedom wrapped his arms around me. "I know you got to do what you feel is the right thing to do."

I allowed myself to relax in his embrace, and as I laid my head on his chest, the tears kept flowing.

CHAPTER 33
STACEY AND RUTH

STACEY AND RUTH rode home in silence. Stacey was shocked at how all this transpired. She was trying to be messy by taking her to see Faith, but something else happened that she had not planned. That was so much better than what she could ever have dreamed. Davis's death drove a deeper wedge between Ruth and Faith while helping them become closer. She placed a hand on Ruth's shoulder. "Ruth, are you okay?"

Ruth touched her hand. "Yes and no. I was not going over to be rude, but sometimes I just could not help myself. I need to be a better person. I need to try to mend this between us; she is all that I have." Ruth began to cry.

"You got me, Miss Ruth. Why are you worried about her? You saw how she treated you in front of her new boyfriend. She doesn't care about you."

Ruth glanced over at me and removed her hand. "I saw her faint, and I saw the pain in her eyes before the officer even told us what had happened to David. It is my fault. I should have stayed home instead of allowing you to talk me into invading her privacy. I should have waited for her to invite me." Ruth continued to cry.

"Well, you didn't, and besides, it isn't your fault that someone had killed him. How did you know that he was going over there?" They had stopped at the stoplight a block from the house.

"I had an idea, and besides, you were pushing it on me."

"So, you trying to say that this is all my fault?" Stacey had turned to face her.

Ruth turned away from her stare. She changed the subject. "I thought she was messing around with Marcus. Where did this guy come from?"

"I said that she slept with him. I never said that that they were together."

Ruth turned her head and looked at the window. "Well, you made it seem like they were going together when you came to my house."

Stacey began to get nervous because she knew that she had to tell another lie for the old lie to stick. "I was upset that day and had no idea what I was going to do. You know how it is when your emotions are all over the place." The light changed to green, and she turned back around to face the street. Stacey kept driving, but out the corner of her eye, she saw Ruth shake her head.

"Miss Ruth, I am here for you, and you do not have to worry about anything I got you!"

Stacey took Ruth's hand into hers. Ruth wanted to snatch it back from her, but she felt Stacey's grip on her hand get tighter, and they rode in silence all the way home.

CHAPTER 34
BETTY

I WAS SO upset when Faith called me and told me that her grandfather had died. Even though she barely spoke about her family, she always talked about how nice he was to her the few times she mentioned him. It had been hard for me to understand what she was saying between her sobs, but I managed to understand her.

But what pissed me off was that when she told me that Stacey was at her house with her mother, I knew something was not right. How the hell could she be with Faith's mom, knowing how that woman had treated her? I could hear the pain coming through the phone, but also sorrow.

I do not even think that she was fully aware of what was going on? I could see that Stacey was playing her mom, lying thru her face about everything. I hated that bitch, and the next time I see her, I will lay her on the ground.

"Who the hell are you talking to?" my husband asked me.

"I'm not talking to anyone," I said. I slipped my phone into my back pocket.

He moved closer to me and got all up in my face. "You better not be talkin' to no dude!"

I stepped away from him. "I'm not like you."

"What the hell do you mean by that?" Greg raised his voice.

I began to get nervous because I knew that at any minute, he would hit me. "Please, baby; it was just Faith. She called me to tell me that her grandfather had died. I didn't mean any harm." I hope that he heard the anguish in my voice. I was pleading with him not to hit me.

"Oh, ok, but why the hell did you lie to me!"

Before I could respond, my husband had raised his arm in the air, and he brought his fist down onto my stomach. I fell to the floor, doubled over in pain. He walked over to me and kicked me in my back. I peed on myself. I felt a sharp pain, and it felt like he had injured my kidneys. I lay on the floor as I watched his feet walk out of the room.

My cell phone began to buzz in my back pocket, and I slowly removed it. I saw that I had a text message from Faith.

I am going to initiate, and I wondered if you could keep an eye on my house. I do not trust Stacey.

I managed to send her a heart emoji, kiss emoji, and a smile emoji with thumbs up.

CHAPTER 35
FAITH

I SAT HOME WAITING ANXIOUSLY for Mama to call with the funeral arrangements. Even though I was not close to his side of the family, I still wanted to be a part of the service. But she never called. I tried calling her, but she would not pick up the phone. I know that we had said some horrible things to one another, but maybe she was still mad with me. We had a death in our family, and we needed to put all this foolishness aside.

When Freedom had finally left, I had tried to do the water thing again. The book called it scrying, and I would ensure that I would not allow fear to stop me this time. I poured the water into the bowl, and I began to concentrate. I moved the water closer to me as I began speaking into the water. I started to feel chills and the whispers began. This time when I heard the voices, I did not stop nor drop the bowl.

At first, it sounded like whispers, but then the voices became one, and it was the sweetest sound that I had ever heard. The sounds were lovely and smooth that it like water.

It sounded like water running smoothly over a babbling brook, and it was so perfect.

"*We are here,*" the voices said.

"What is wrong with me?" I asked them.

"Nothing you need to allow us to help you and allow us to guide you," they answered.

"I lost my grandfather, and now I have no idea what is going on with the funeral. I do not even know where it is going to be. No one is calling me, and I feel all alone." I began to cry, and my cries turned into heavy sobs. I was feeling helpless and exhausted.

"Cry for as the water flows from your eyes, it is healing for your soul, for your *kra*." I cried until I could not cry anymore, and some of my tears fell into the bowl. When I stopped crying, I asked them about the word that they had said. I heard Nana mention the same word to me. "My what?"

"*Your kra. Soon all will be revealed to you, and you will understand who you are and what you are.*"

"What am I? I do not understand what you are saying to me. Am I not Faith? Am I not Ruth's daughter? Am I a threat to the ones that I love?" I waited for a response, but none came. After five minutes of waiting and trying to get the voices to speak again, I placed the bowl down on the table and went upstairs to lay down. I was so tired. All I wanted to do was go to sleep and not wake up until all the drama was over.

But then it hit me. I needed to call and tell Betty. She was my real friend, and I knew she would be there for me no matter what. We spoke briefly, but before she hung up the phone, I heard her sorry-ass husband in the background yelling at her. I waited a few minutes before I called her back. I knew that she had to handle what she needed to with him, so I texted her. I did not trust Stacey anymore. I needed Betty to keep an eye on my house while I initiated.

THE DESTRUCTION OF FAITH

She texts me back all these emojis, which let me know that she was unable to talk. I swear to god that once this is over, I will write a poem about his ass!

CHAPTER 36
RUTH

RUTH HAD RECEIVED several phone calls from David's sisters telling her about the funeral. They wanted Faith to come and read the obituary, but she had said that Faith did not want to do it. Even though Ruth knew that Faith would have accepted the invitation to do something for him, it was her who did not wish Faith to do it. She had told them that she would not be able to attend the funeral and that she and Faith would send some flowers.

Ruth never did like her step-aunts anyway. To her, they always were so bougie and acted like she was a pest. They never gave her any presents for Christmas. She missed out on all her birthdays, and they never really did like her mother. Hell, Ruth never liked her mother. But she could never figure out why they hated her mother so much?

According to David's last request, he wanted a quick ceremony after he died. He did not want people standing around in sorrow, but he wanted to rejoice in his life. He desired cremation. He wanted his family to enjoy the money left in his life insurance policy and be happy. He had taken out two separate policies. One of his sisters had told her that he had left everything to Faith on one of his policies. His sister said to her that they did not need anything else.

Ruth could not believe it, but after all, that was the least that he could have done for not helping them out when he was alive. David's sister had told Ruth that she needed to be at the lawyer's office on Monday morning to go over the rest of David's estate, for there was more in the will. Ruth asked for the amount, and she almost fell out of her chair when she revealed it to her. Faith inherited his life's savings plus money from his life insurance policy, totaling nearly a million dollars.

Stacey had run into the living room when she heard Ruth cry out. When Ruth hung up the phone, she told Stacey that Faith was a millionaire. The blood in Stacey's body began to boil with jealousy. But she had to let that reside for now. Her mission to destroy Faith had somewhat changed; for now, she began plotting how she would get her hands on that money.

CHAPTER 37
ARE YOU READY?

FRIDAY HAD FINALLY MADE it to me, and I contemplated if I wanted to do this initiation. I was having second thoughts now. I called Nana to tell her that I had a death in my family, and she informed me that it was the best time to take the initiation because it would help revere him to the ancestor's realm. I still had so many unanswered questions that I did not have a chance to ask Freedom when he was here. But just like that, he was here knocking on my door.

I ran downstairs in the nude and opened the door. Freedom's eyes immediately went to my breasts.

"You know you are a lovely woman, " he said smiling. He was holding two cups in his hands from Smoothie King,

"Come on in," I said, walking back upstairs to put on some clothes.

When I came back downstairs, he was taking off his shoes and sitting on the pillows. "I hope you like mango," he said.

"Yes, I love mango."

He reached on the table and handed me the smoothie.

I took a sip. "This taste so good." I took another sip.

"Well, you know today is your big day, and Nana asked me

THE DESTRUCTION OF FAITH

to come and pick you up. She said that your mind needs to be free without any distraction, so here I am."

"Wait, I thought that you were against me doing this?"

"Baby, that has not changed, but I am here for you like I told you earlier." He sipped on his smoothie. "Oh, by the way, do you have any problems with them cutting your hair?"

"Wait, what?" My hair is going to get cut?" I had no idea that I had to cut my hair, and he called me baby.

"Yep, all of it. I mean, you already got the sides shaved, so why not cut it all off?"

"But what about my locs? I mean, it took me forever to get them to this length?"

"Snip, snip," he said, making the cutting gesture with his fingers.

"I do not know about this."

"Vanity is a foolish thing to have. Trust me, your hair will grow back so fast, and it will contain the *ashe* of the spirits in it."

"It may not be so bad; I do have a lot of negative energy in my hair." I thought for a moment. "So, is there anything else that I need to know?"

"Well, I see that you have tattoos, which means that you are not afraid of some pain. So you must know that they will be making small cuts all over your back."

"Get the fuck out of her! Really?"

"Back out now if you are skirmish," he managed to say thru his laughter. He was laughing so hard at me.

"I do not know if I can do all of this." I was shaking my head.

"Come Faith, I have told you too much now. I was just trying to scare you to stop you, but I am sorry, your back will be beautiful." He kissed me on my cheek.

When his lips touched my face, I thought I was going to melt. His lips were so soft, and I felt a coolness on them.

Suddenly I felt a cool breeze, and it felt familiar. I had felt this before but could not remember where. Freedom was staring at me. I watched his eyes move from eyes and glance to my lips. Slowly I parted lips, thinking he was about to kiss me. I needed him so badly. But he held back.

"Before we leave the house, what else do I need to know? Do I need to bring something?" I stood back from him. I wanted to throw him on the floor and ride him.

"Nope, just yourself." Freedom said. He was putting his shoes on.

"Come now; there got to be something else that you are not telling me?"

"I have told you everything that you need to know right now. Like I said, my job is to protect you and keep you safe, and that is all that you need to know."

But I felt that he was not telling me everything I needed to know.

CHAPTER 38
INITIATION

WHEN WE DROVE up into the bookstore's parking lot, I noticed that someone had parked their car right in front of the store. It had out-of-state tags on it. This person driving the vehicle was from D.C. Freedom parked beside the car, and then he got out and walked around to my side of the vehicle. I watched him, wondering what he was doing. He opened my door and extended his hand out to me. I smiled. I hope that others were watching him treat me like a queen. He held my hand as he helped me out of the car, and I saw Yemi standing near the door.

As soon as she saw us walk up, she opened the door. She was wearing all white. "I am so excited for you," she whispered as I walked past her.

"Thank you," I whispered back. I was still holding Freedom's hand and wearing my smile.

Freedom escorted me thru the bookstore and the center. I saw some people sitting in there. "Who are they?" I asked him. We walked past him.

"They are part of the shrine, but the one in D.C. They are here to witness your initiation."

We walked thru the door I had seen Nana come out from during the festival. He escorted me thru the door and led me down these stairs into this small room. *I did not even know that she had a basement in this building.* A small cot and a large wooden basin filled with water and herbs were in the middle of this room. I could hear soft African drumming music coming from somewhere inside the room.

Red and yellow candles lighted the room. The shadows from the flickering flames were dancing off the walls. It reminded me of the Princess and the Frog scene when the voodoo man sang his song. And as he sang, the shadows danced around him. I saw a small table with white clothing on it. There was also this white bowl sitting there that looked like white powder was in it. I also noticed a small brown mat lying on the floor. The room had a small door, and we heard three knocks. The door opened, and Nana walked in with this older woman.

The older woman introduced herself. "My name is Nana Afua. I am here to assist Nana Madou with your rites of passage."

I bowed my head to her, but I did not try to touch her hand.

"This is Faith," Nana said, introducing us. From what I was gathering from their body movements, Nana Afua was over Nana Madou, for she stood slightly behind Nana Afua after they had entered the room.

Nana Afua looked at Freedom and spoke. "You can go back and energize."

I watched how Freedom nodded his head to her, but his eyes were sending her another message. Nana Afua bowed her head slightly as he passed her. That was weird, and I made a mental note to ask him about that gesture later. Once he left the room, Nana Madou diverted her attention back to me.

THE DESTRUCTION OF FAITH

"Now, daughter," she said to me. "I call you daughter because I am about to be your spiritual mother. I need you to undress and remove all types of jewelry you have, including your tongue and belly rings. Once you do that, I need you to step into this water and wash your body with the herbs. They will cleanse all the negativity from you. I am going to leave this bell here for you to ring after you bathe, lay down on the mat on your stomach with your hands and arms placed beside you."

Before I could respond, she and Nana Afua had left the room. I wanted to tell her that I was nervous, and I hoped that the markings that would cut my back would not hurt. I removed all my clothes as she had instructed, including all my jewelry. I stepped in the water, and it was exactly right. Very warm and comforting. I used the cup that was placed in the water and began to pour the water on me. I started from the top of my head and enjoyed the water as it flowed down my body. I do not know what herbs they had added to the water, but they smelled so sweet, so I repeated that process twice.

I did not see a towel that I could use, so I laid across the mat when I got out and rang the bell. Both women came in, and I saw Nana Madou carrying a small silver plate with a silver chalice and several razors. Nana Afua was holding a pair of scissors with a towel draped across her right shoulder. They both knelt to my level. Nana Afua used the towel to pat dry by back off. Neither of the women said a word as they began working on me.

The first cut she made stung a little, but it didn't hurt as bad as I thought. I did not wince, and this must not have been acceptable, for the next cut was a little deeper into my flesh, and I winced then. They must've noticed how I was tensing up but chose to ignore me. After the tenth cut, my back, for some reason, began to become numb. I could no longer feel the razor cutting into my flesh. I closed my eyes as I smelled the scent of Kush in the room.

Nana Afua took the towel and placed it across my back. She was blotting my back to remove the blood, and then she muttered something in a different language as she slowly and gently removed the towel. I turned my head to get a glimpse of the bloody towel, and I was shocked. Did I even bleed? Both women gave each a short nod, and Nana Afua placed the towel on the table. Nana Madou gestured for me to sit up, and she began cutting off my locs.

As my locs began to fall from my head, I closed my eyes because I did not want to see my hair falling on the floor. It felt like something was being removed from me as each loc fell to the floor. The drumming music was still playing in the room, and I became more relaxed as they continued to work on me. I wanted to fall asleep, but my eyes would not close. I was no longer smelling Kush, but I was relaxed, and I had never felt this way before, not even when I was getting high. Even when I was doing mushrooms, my soul was floating around me, and I watched it move around the room.

When the women finished working on me, they told me to stand up and brush my hair. Nana Madou took a bowl from under the table that contained crushed herbs. I had not seen that. She told me to stand still as she packed each cut with the crushed spices. I thought it would sting, but even though I was burning, I was not feeling anything.

After adding the spices to my cuts, Nan Afua grabbed the white cloth from the table and wrapped it around my body. I thought they had just been white clothes, not fabric. She took a belt and tied it around my waist to keep the cloth around me. Next, they placed two beaded anklets on my ankles. They also put two beaded necklaces around my neck. I wished to see what I looked like, but I could not look in the mirror at my reflection.

THE DESTRUCTION OF FAITH

Nana Afua instructed me to sit on the floor while she held my head, and Nana Madou used the clippers to shave my hair down some more. I had not seen the clippers earlier, just the scissors. She then took a fresh razor from the plate and made seven cuts into the top of my head. They asked me to stick out my tongue, and she made three cuts on my tongue. Nana placed herbs in my mouth as well into the cuts on my head. I did not feel those cuts either.

"Stand up," Nana Madou commanded.

I stood up while Nana Afua took me by the hands and guided me out of the room. They told me to keep my eyes closed as I felt led down the hallway up the stairs and back into this open space. *I must be back in the center.* Yes, I am in the center because I can smell that wonderful incense. My eyes remained close because they told me they wanted to know I could follow instructions to keep my eyes closed on my own. If I kept my eyes closed without peeking, that meant that I would not tell their secrets.

They begin taking me somewhere. Nana Afua helps me walk up the stairs, and I guess that I am in the center. And they help me take a seat on a small stool that one of them guides me to. I take a seat. I am still feeling euphoric as I hear the drumming music, and my body is so relaxed. I wonder if I am near the veil. Hopefully, I will go behind the veil and see what is in the earthen pot.

Someone moved past me, and I felt them lightly brush against my leg. I hear a slight clinking sound by my feet. I can smell something like cinnamon coming from whatever they placed near my feet. Someone lifted my feet and put them in this basin. The water feels cool. When my feet touched the bottom of the bowl, I felt something like shells underneath them. The bowl is then pushed closer towards the stool, and before they push it under there, my feet are removed and wiped off.

Next, I feel something like a fire around my face. Whomever it moves it around, it seems like the fire is getting too close to my face, and I gasp. Someone taps me hard on my arm because I still have the herbs in my mouth, and I cannot speak yet. I regain my composure and get serious. The heat from the flames has caused my flesh to become extremely hot. I want to open my eyes to see what is going on. What is in that fire? My skin feels like it is burning! They stopped twirling the flames around me, and I began to feel this painful sensation, unlike the cuts made into my body. But I did not feel any tingling in the back of my neck. Either Bella was asleep, or she knew that no one was harming me.

Then it felt like somebody had turned on a fan, and it was blowing across my body and cooling me off. I could not hear a fan blowing, but it had to be a fan because the breeze was strong. It was fantastic, and it reminded me of Freedom's kiss.

After completing that part of the ritual, someone took my hands and placed these beaded bracelets on them. I kept my eyes closed as no one touched me for what seemed like forever. Finally, I felt someone standing behind me, and I could smell a hint of Kush. It smelled like the scent that Freedom was wearing earlier. I began to relax even more because I knew that he was standing behind me. He did tell me that he was here to protect me.

Nana Madou was standing in front of me, for she told me to open my mouth and spit into something. I spit the herbs out of my mouth, and my tongue felt normal. Before the cuts, she had begun chanting over me in a different language. It was *Twi* in which I later found out was the language of the Ghana people. Whatever she was chanting around me now was causing me to become dizzy, but I could still smell his scent.

THE DESTRUCTION OF FAITH

The more she began speaking in *Twi,* the more I understood what she was saying to me.

"*Daughters rise amongst the spirits who have been waiting for you. The great mother calls you as the sun greets the moon and the water greets the earth, Behold the daughter, behold the life, behold the goddess.*"

My head began pounding like never before. I also started feeling tingling in the back of my neck now. Was *she* becoming upset? It was making me nervous, for I felt safe. I knew that she would show herself, or this spirit would take me over. I could smell Freedom's scent, and I wanted to reach out to him, but my arms felt weightless. I could not raise them even if I wanted to. What were they doing to me, and what was in those herbs?

Nana Madou placed a set of beads around my neck and kissed me on the forehead, but it was not her lips. They belonged to Freedom. I knew his touch.

"Open your eyes," Nana Madou instructed.

I opened them, but to my surprise, no one was standing in front of me. I turned my head around, and no one was standing behind me. I knew that it was not all in my mind. I knew what I was smelling and feeling concerning Freedom, but where was he? I did not see him, but I could still smell him around me. I was sitting directly beside the veil, and only women were standing in front of me a few feet away. They were all dressed like I was, and it was apparent that they were initiates as well.

At least I had not been the only one sitting here half naked with nothing but a white cloth covering me. I felt like I had just become a part of sisterhood as I had finally become part of a family, and at this very moment, I was genuinely happy. They all began to crowd around me, welcoming me into their family. I tried to see past them, for I still smelt Freedom's scent.

CHAPTER 39
STACEY IS UP TO NO GOOD

STACEY HAD DRIVEN over to Faith's house to see if she was at home. She wanted to tell her the good news, that she had just inherited a lot of money. She knew that Faith could not resist playing with her sexually, so all she had to do was seduce her, and she would be sharing all Faith's wealth.

She knocked on the door, but no one answered. She walked around the side of the house and saw Faith's car parked in the back of the house. She walked around to the back of the house because maybe Faith was like her mother and kept the back door open. *Yep, just like her mom.* She opened the door and tried to go in. But something was wrong.

Every time she tried to place her foot on the step to walk through the threshold, it felt like an invisible barrier preventing her from entering the house. She kept trying to force herself inside the house. During her last attempt, a strong force knocked her on her ass.

What the hell was going on?

She picked herself up from the ground and walked back around to the front of the house. Whatever Faith had to go

THE DESTRUCTION OF FAITH

on in that house was not allowing her to come in. She pulled her cell phone out of her bag and dialed Faith's number. The phone was ringing, and she could hear it from outside. "Faith!" she shouted. "I know that you are in there. Please open the door because I have something to tell you!"

She waited. Faith still did not come to the door. Maybe she was asleep. She took a piece of paper, wrote her a note, and left it under the windshield wiper on her car. When she got up and decided to leave out, she would see the message and call her. Stacey's phone began ringing, and she saw that it was Ruth, she answered the phone, "Hi Miss Ruth, what's up?"

"How long will it take you to get here? I need to go to the store, and I was wondering if you could take me?" Ruth said.

Damn, how was she getting around before I came?

"Sure, I will be there in 15 minutes," she said. She hung up the phone. Ruth was so stupid and crazy as hell. Stacy could see why Faith had to get out of there. Pretty soon, it would be over, and she would no longer be playing that role of liking her and being her fake daughter.

CHAPTER 40
BETTY

I HAD PULLED up in front of Faith's house, and I saw Stacey walking up to the house. I had spoken to Faith earlier. Even though she had texted me and told me to watch her house, I still wanted to make sure; besides, I knew Faith was doing something special today, and she was not home. I watched as Stacey walked to the back of the house after not answering the front door.

What was Stacey doing?

I was about to dial Faith's number and let her know that Stacey was creeping around her home. I hoped that she had her cell phone with her. But something told me not to call her. The last time we spoke face-to-face, Faith said that she did not want anything to do with Stacey. She said that she would let Stacey eat her out, but that was all that would occur. Even the thought of Stacey going down on my best friend was disgusting but to each their own. I watched Stacey walk back around the house and sit down on the porch. She was on her phone, and I wondered with whom she was having a conversation.

I decided that I was going to follow her. Something was

THE DESTRUCTION OF FAITH

not sitting right with me, and I wanted to know what Stacey was doing. I followed her at least two cars back as I saw her driving toward Faith's mother's house. Stacey pulled up in the driveway and got out of the vehicle. I watched as Stacey took out her key and used it to open the front door.

What the fuck? What is she doing with keys to Faith's mother's house?

She went inside the house. A few minutes later, I saw Ruth and Stacey come out of the house to get into Stacey's car. They were laughing and acting like they were close. But then a thought occurred, was Stacey living there? I didn't particularly appreciate watching the two of them carry on like that. I needed to tell Faith, but I needed more proof. What the hell was Stacey doing with a key to Ruth's house, and why were they acting like the perfect mother and daughter? I knew that the back door was open, so as soon as I saw them drive off, I snuck in the back door to see what was going on.

As soon as I opened the door, the house smelled of marijuana and stale cigarettes. I walked around the kitchen then entered the living room, searching for clues. For a few minutes, after not finding anything, I started going down the hallway. As I walked down the hallway, I smelled that oil that Stacey was always wearing, and it was intense. I pinched my nose because I was not too fond of that scent.

I decided to go into Faith's old room to see if her mother had changed anything, and damn was I surprised at what I saw! No more speculating. I had all my answers. It looked like Stacey was living here because I saw her clothes strewn all over the place, and there sat a bottle of Egyptian Musk sitting on the mantle. Shit, I cannot wait to tell Faith. I had all the proof that I needed. She is going to beat the brakes off Stacey's ass! Better yet, I hope she writes a poem about her.

As I turned around to leave the room, I heard voices

come from the living room. They were back. I began to get nervous because I did not want to get caught.

"I'm sorry, Stacey," I heard Miss Ruth say. "My head started hurting, and I just needed to come home. Maybe tomorrow we can go to the store."

"It's alright, Miss Ruth," I heard Stacey reply. "I have nothing planned for tomorrow. Why not you just lay down, and I will be right here when you wake up. I know that you have a lot on your plate with David dying and all and then leaving all that money to Faith."

"Yes, I do. Faith is a millionaire, and she doesn't even know it."

I covered my mouth to stop myself from being heard as I gasped. That conniving bitch! No wonder she was living over; I knew that she was up to something. I bet Miss Ruth is plotting on that money too.

"And I want you to stop calling me Miss Ruth. I wish you would start calling me mom because I see you like my daughter, and you have done more for me than my daughter has ever done."

"*Mom,* I am just so glad that you allowed me to stay here after she had slept with Marcus. We should not tell her about her inheritance."

"What you mean about that?" Miss Ruth said. "I have to tell her. Hopefully, she will give me some of the money."

I heard Stacey laugh. "Fait is not going to give you shit! Remember what she said to you when we went over there. She hates you!"

I heard sniffle sounds coming from Miss Ruth. She must be crying.

"Stop crying, Mom. You got me, and I will make sure that you are straight."

They must've hugged each other, for no one spoke for a

THE DESTRUCTION OF FAITH

few seconds. Then I heard Miss Ruth reply," Thank God for you, Stacey. I am so glad that you are in my life."

Stacey then replied, "Fuck that trifling bitch! I hate her for sleeping with Marcus behind my back."

That is when I could not take anymore, and I ran out of Faith's room screaming at them. I ran into the living room, and they were sitting together on the couch. "How dare you lie on Faith like that, and you live here? Wait until I tell Faith what you two been doing!"

"What the fuck are you doing in my house," Ruth yelled. "You are an intruder!"

"I was following Stacey. I was at Faith's house when she pulled up, and something told me to follow her to see what she was doing. Now I am glad that I did!" I glanced over at Stacey and lashed out at her. "You were never her friend! Then you going to lie on her to her mother and say that she slept with Marcus?"

"Betty, calm down; it's not what you think," Stacey said in a calming tone.

"What is she talking about?" Miss Ruth said.

"Do not pay any attention to her. She did not know," Stacey replied.

"Don't pay any attention to me!" I screamed. "I cannot wait to tell Faith what I heard and saw. You know this will devastate her if she found out that you were living here with her mother and telling lies about her!" I knew that Faith wanted to mess with Marcus to get back at her, but she never followed through with it. And if she did fuck him, Stacey deserved it.

"What Faith don't know will not hurt her," Stacey spat at me.

"We will see," I stated.

I turned my back to them to leave the house. As I was

walking towards the front door, I could hear Stacey yelling at me to stop. I stopped walking and turned around. Stacey hit me in the head with a vase that was sitting on the table. I did not see in her hands. I fell forward, landing on the couch. My head hit the corner of the chair as I fell. The blow had knocked me out.

"Did you kill her?" Ruth said. She was hysterical.

"Nope, I think I just knocked her out," Stacey said, huffing and puffing like she was all out of breath.

"You need to kill her because she broke into my house! She probably stole something from the back rooms while we were gone!" Ruth said. She was excited now, and she had forgotten all about that headache.

No matter how bad Stacey was, she was not a murderer. "I do not want to kill Betty."

After a few minutes, I began stirring, trying to wake up. I opened my eyes and touched my head. When I pulled my hand back, there was blood on my fingers. I was in a lot of pain and very dizzy. I tried to stand up, and that is when I saw Ruth pick up that glass ashtray. I was trying to get up because I knew what she was about to do, but I was so dizzy. I knew then that it was over for me as she swung her arms high in the air and came down hard against my skull.

Ruth hit Betty in the head several times with that glass ashtray until parts of Betty's brain were splattered all over the floor. Ruth kept smashing into her skull, and with each blow, she cursed Faith, blaming her for her shitty life. When she tired herself out, Ruth stood up and dropped the ashtray. Betty's blood was on her and the floor.

"Ruth, why the hell did you do that?" Stacey said. Stacey did not want to kill anyone. She knew that she should have stopped her but watching Betty die had been so beautiful.

"Because I wanted to! She will go back and tell Faith what she heard us say, and I will never get my daughter back!"

"What do you mean by getting your daughter back? The

THE DESTRUCTION OF FAITH

only reason you want to play nice is so that she will give you some of the money that she had inherited!" Stacey screamed at her. She got in Ruth's face. Stacey could not believe that Ruth still had some feelings for her daughter.

"If I were you, little girl, I would back the fuck up and remember who the fuck you talking to!" Ruth stared her down.

Stacey blinked her eyes as if she had forgotten what she had just witnessed. She calmed her voice down and backed up. There was no telling what this crazy woman would do to her. Now she saw she knew what Faith had been going through. She had to change the energy real quick before Ruth hit her. "I apologize, but why did you kill Betty? When Faith finds out, it will be over for the both of us."

Ruth giggled. "How is she going to know? Are you going to tell her?"

Stacey shook her head. "No, I am not going to tell her, but she has a way of finding out things. I am going to have to come up with something to tell her about Betty."

"Just shut the fuck up and help me move the body."

Stacey stared at Ruth as if she were crazy. Had Ruth killed before?

CHAPTER 41
FAITH

I WAS SO hungry when the initiation was over. All I wanted to do was go home and eat that meal that I did not get to eat with my grandfather. Freedom had stored it away in the refrigerator. I had finally seen Freedom after Nana Madou took me to that room to put on my clothes. When we walked back into the center, he stood near the veil and walked over to me. He told me that he was going to drive me home. Of course, Nana Madou kept insisting that I stay there, but I wanted to go home. My eye was twitching, and I knew that something still was not right. I had no idea what was going on, but I preferred to be at home. She said that she understood, and Freedom escorted me outside. I noticed some energy transpire between them, but I said nothing. My head was beginning to hurt.

Freedom walked me to the car and opened the door. I smiled at him. Once I got into the car, I leaned my head back against the seat. I felt so drained, but I still had a few questions to ask him. I waited for him to get in the vehicle.

"I smelled that scent that you be wearing during my initiation. The first time I smelled it, I was lying on my back while

THE DESTRUCTION OF FAITH

Nana and the other lady were making those incisions. Then I smelt it again in the center. I even felt you kiss me on the forehead, but when I was allowed to open my eyes, you were nowhere around. Please explain that." I ended.

Freedom started the car and pulled out of the parking lot. When we got a block away from the bookstore, he pulled the car over into Bojangles parking lot and turned it off. "Faith, there is a lot about me that you do not know. I want to tell you so much, but right now, I am not allowed to."

I looked at him. "What do you mean you are not allowed?"

"You just been through your rites of passage, and I am not allowed to speak to you about spiritual matters right now. You experience my energy being around you before, and you correlate my scent to your comfort and security. My scent makes you feel safe, and it's like a security blanket. You needed to feel safe, and hence you began to smell me."

It sounded like he was feeding me bullshit. I was a little confused, but maybe he was right. "I guess you are right, Freedom. I did need to feel safe and secure. You know, it felt like Nana was trying to cut something out of me. She was digging deep in my flesh, and it was hurting. That was when I smelt you, and my back got numb."

Freedom reached over with his hand as if he would grab my hand; then, he pulled back. "I cannot touch you right now, but I do feel that you will understand everything very quickly. But may I ask you one thing?"

"Sure, Freedom, what is it?" I heard a seriousness in his voice.

"Can you promise me that no matter what happens that you will not allow anyone to take your power? That you will keep being who you are and not become a slave to the religion?"

Where was he heading to with that question? I had no

intention of being a slave for no one, especially to religion. "I promise," I answered.

Freedom smiled and blew me a kiss. "Let's get out of here before I get some of that chicken." I smiled at him. I was ready to go home.

He had driven me home and had wanted to stay. I told him that I just needed to rest and get myself together. My back felt a little sore, but my tongue was not all swollen from the cuts.

I walked into the house and went into the kitchen to grab the food from the fridge. As I placed the food on the kitchen counter, I glanced out the window. I noticed that there was a piece of paper on the windshield of my car, so I went outside to get it. It was a note from Stacey telling me to give her a call.

Not tonight, I thought to myself because I was exhausted.

I walked back into the house and went and got my cell phone. I saw that I had several missed calls from Stacey. Damn, she was blowing me up. I needed to call Betty to see if she knew why Stacey had been at my house. I knew that she was going to try something. I dialed her number, but it went straight to voice mail. I also wanted to share my experience with her. I hoped that her husband had not be beating on her again. I called her phone again, but I got no answer. It went straight to voice mail, and I left her a message. I also saw that Mama had called me too. I checked my voicemail she had left a message telling me that we had to talk about something serious.

What the hell was going?

I dialed her number, and she answered on the first ring. "Ma, what's up?"

"Nothing, baby," my mother said, sounding all sweet.

She had never sounded this sweet before.

"What are you doing, baby?"

THE DESTRUCTION OF FAITH

Now she is calling me baby. Something must be going on with her. "Nothing, I just did this initiation, and I will come to see you and talk to you about it."

"What kind of initiation?" I could hear that judgmental tone back in her voice.

"Ma, are you okay." I was not ready for her mess, especially after what I had experienced tonight.

"Can you stop by here in the morning?" her voice sounded all sugary. She was hopeful.

"Sure, ma, I will be there in the morning." I hung up the phone.

What was going on?

I went back to warming up and my food, and I felt a strange but familiar presence in my house. I smelled Kush, and I thought that Freedom had just ignored what I wanted and come back, but he was not there when I walked into the living room.

I must be tired.

I sat down on the pillow to eat my food. The moment that I tried to taste the food; the food did not taste right. Maybe it was the cuts on my tongue and those herbs. I got up and walked back into the kitchen. I put the plate into the sink, walked back into the living room, turned off the lights, and went upstairs. I was too drained to eat anyway. The scent of Kush was lingering in the air, and I ignored it. I lay across my bed and fell asleep.

CHAPTER 42
FREEDOM

FREEDOM SAT IN THE CAR, waiting for Faith to turn the lights off. Faith had no idea how badly he wanted to stay. She was so different, so strong, so sexy, but yet he could not have her. He had wished that she had not taken that initiation, for certain things were prohibited within the Akan ways. But she took it anyway, and all he could do was be there for her.

Freedom was not going to violate any unspoken rules, but he craved Faith. Her essence was pure but full of pain and sorrow. He wanted to take her away from this world and keep her to himself. He was very selfish with his women.

When Nana Madou began cutting into her back, he knew why she was cutting deep. She wanted to make that spirit come forth and take it for herself. Freedom knew that *Bella* inhabited her, what Faith called her. *Bella* was a force to be reckoned with, and she was the one who empowered her with her gifts. But Faith had no idea what she housed. Many names had known *Bella*, and Nana Madou wanted her.

Freedom had heard her wince, and he just wanted to calm her and take her mind off the pain. He was able to move in and out of certain places. He could go where no human could go, and he was more potent than Faith knew. His job was to protect her, but his protection over her was turning into much more.

Faith was connecting with him because she could smell him, and no other woman had ever been able to connect to his scent. He hated lying to her, but soon she would know the truth, and he hoped that she would be able to handle it. He watched as the lights went out and drove off deep in his thoughts.

CHAPTER 43
BETTY IS NOT DEAD

THE FOLLOWING DAY, I awoke with a loud knocking on my door. I ran downstairs and snatched the door open. It was Stacey.

"What the fuck do you want!" I said to her.

"Did you see the news?" She was acting like she was nervous, and it looked like she had been crying.

"I have been sleeping. Besides, you know that I do not own a television so tell me what is happening." I let her come in.

She pulled out her phone and found the app for the WRAL news station. The first thing that I saw was a picture of Betty flashing across her screen. "What is going on?"

"They found her body behind Hunter Elementary School. She is dead."

I fell against the wall. There was no way that my best friend was dead.

"They say that it looked like foul play and that her husband is the prime suspect. They say that because they found evidence of old bruise marks on her body." Stacey said.

"No, Stacey! No!" I cried. "This cannot be true. I told

Betty to leave him because I felt like something would happen to her if she stayed with him. Last night my eye was twitching, and I knew something bad was going to happen!" Tears began streaming down my face, and I was hurt but angry.

"Faith, what happened to your hair?" Stacey said, staring at me all funny.

I looked at her. "How can you stand there and ask me about my hair? You got to be kidding me! My best friend is dead, and all you are concerned about is my hair? That will grow back, but Betty is never coming back!"

I walked into the living room and sat down on the floor. Stacey walked into the house and closed the door behind her. She then followed me into the living room. " I need for you to tell me exactly what the news station is saying."

"Well, from what I gathered, she had not been seen since yesterday, and the husband had called the police to file a missing report. A cop was working around Hunter, and he drove behind the school. He saw Betty's car parked behind there running, and when he approached it, he saw Betty lying in the passenger's side with her head bashed in. She was dead."

The tears stopped flowing from my eyes, and I began to feel numb. Betty had been the only person I knew without a shadow of a doubt had my back, and now she was gone. First my grandfather and now my best friend. I grabbed the book from the shelf and began flipping the pages. *What was I doing?* I never wrote a poem about her dying, so I knew that it was not my fault. I threw my book against the wall. I wish Freedom had stayed the night. Right now, I needed him.

"You still didn't tell me what happened to your hair," Stacey said again.

I could not believe that Stacey was still worrying about my hair. But of course, she never really did care too much about Betty. Stacey always said negative things about her to get me to stop being her friend. She had even accused us of sleeping together. I did not want to get into that conversation with her concerning my hair, not right now. She was standing over me, acting like she was concerned. The back of my head began to tingle. I looked up at her. "I was all cut off for initiation. I initiated into the Akan religion last night."

"The Akan religion? What does that mean?" she asked.

She was getting on my damn nerves. "Look, I do not want to discuss this with you. I need to go to see my mother, and I need to see Betty's mother. I know she is devastated because they were so close. Don't you have a heart? I used to wish that I were close to my mom like she was."

Stacey was trying her best to be supportive, but she couldn't.

Stacey just stared at me, and then it hit me that she was glad that Betty was no longer here. She was pretending to care.

"Are you glad that Betty is dead? You are acting like you do not care about what happened to her?"

Stacey flopped down beside me on the pillows and tried to embrace me. I pushed her away from me. She stood back up. "Do you need me to take you to your mom's house?"

She does not care, but I could not argue with her. I was not in the right frame of mind to drive. "Can you? I am not in the mood to be driving." I was still in my street clothes from last night, so I grabbed a scarf to cover my hair and left with her.

On the drive to my mother's house, all I could do was think about Betty and grandaddy. I had just lost the two most influential people in my life, and how was I going to be able to heal from this? It felt like I was on an emotional rollercoaster, and it just kept going down with no end to this ride.

CHAPTER 44
CONFRONTATION

WHEN WE ARRIVED at my mother's house, I noticed a gray Camry parked in the yard beside the house. *Who was that?* We entered the house, and my mother was sitting there with two old ladies from the church. They were clasping their bibles as if they were afraid.

"Hey Faith, how you been?" one of the ladies asked me.

"I am ok," I told her, then I looked at mother. "Mom, do you still need to talk to me?"

"Yes, these ladies are mothers from the church. I asked them to come over here to help me pray for you," she said. There was no anger in her voice.

Why did she sound all sweet?

"Look, I do not need any prayer from you or anyone else. I thought you had something significant to tell me. Stacey, can you please take me home?" I could not believe that this woman had me come over here for a prayer meeting.

Stacey was no longer standing beside me. *Where had she run off too?* I called out to her. "Stacey, where you at?"

"Coming," I heard her say. But it sounded like she was in my old bedroom. I walked past my mother and those ladies from her church and went to my room. I opened the door, and Stacey was sitting on my bed, surrounded by her things.

I began to feel a pounding in my head and tingling in the back of my neck. *Bella* was waking up. I thought that she had left, for I had not felt her strongly since the initiation. As my head began to pound, my heartbeat faster due to the anger rising in me. I could feel the adrenaline rushing, and I did not like the thoughts entering my mind. "What the fuck is going on?" I asked her in a calm voice. I was trying not to show my emotions.

"I was going to tell you, but you weren't home last night when I dropped by," Stacey said.

"Tell me what?" I knew that it was going to be another lie coming out of her mouth.

"Faith, I left Marcus because I found out that he had been sleeping with this woman on his job, and I could not take it anymore. I came over here when I could not get an answer from you, and your mother let me stay here."

Stacey was lying to me. It looked like she had been living here for longer than one night. "I do not believe anything that comes out of your mouth. You have this life with my mother so stay the fuck away from me!" I needed to get out of there before *Bella* emerged, and I knew that the anger I was feeling was not residing. I did not want to hurt anyone. I could not take the betrayal from her any longer. I ran out of the room headed towards the living room.

As I moved towards the front door, one of the church ladies was blocking me from leaving. She had her arms held high, and she was waving her bible at me.

"You can't leave Faith. Let us help you," she said to me.

"Move out my way," I said to her. I was still trying to remain calm because I knew that I would erupt if I did not. She just stood there watching me, and then she began chanting the *Lord's Prayer* under her breath.

THE DESTRUCTION OF FAITH

I ran to the back door, and the other lady from church blocked that. I wanted to push her out the way, but I respected my elders. "Can you please move out of my way?" I pleaded with her.

She just stood there with her eyes closed, rocking back and forth. She was clutching her bible tightly to her chest.

What in the hell was my mother planning on doing to me?

The next thing I knew, I felt my mother and the other church lady place their hands on me, and they were dragging me towards the living room. I was screaming and trying to break free from their hold, but they were a lot stronger than I thought. I almost fell to the floor, but they held on tight to me. The pain in my head was more significant now, and I knew that if they did not let me go, someone would get hurt.

They dragged me back into the living room, and Stacey was sitting on the couch staring at me as if she did not care what would happen to me. I began directing my anger towards her. "I trusted you, Stacey. I knew that I should have completely ended our friendship. But once again, you betrayed me."

"It's not what you think," Stacey said. She was pretending to remain calm. " I had nothing to do with this. I had no idea that your mother was planning an intervention. I am sorry Faith," I could Stacey blink her eyes, trying to make fake tears form in them as she spoke to me.

I was no longer believing anything that she had to say. "Stop with the fake tears. You better be glad that they are holding me right now! When I get loose, I am going to beat the shit out of you! You knew what my mother was planning, you connive bitch!"

"Faith, I love you! I did not know what she was going to do. But you do need help, so please calm down. " Stacey pleaded with me.

Maybe she didn't know, but she still betrayed me.

"How can you love her when she slept with your man?" my mother asked. My mother had a puzzled look. "You still want to be friends with after she slept with Marcus? What is going on, Stacey?"

"What! I have never slept with Marcus! Is that what you told my mom to get over here?" The women from the church eased up on their hold. I was livid; how could she lie on me like that. What did I have that she wanted so badly? I did not have shit, and she had more than I could ever have. I was never jealous of her. She wore all the best clothes, and she got whatever she wanted; her family had spoiled her.

"Stacey told me that she caught you two together and that she needed a place to stay, so I allowed her to stay here," my mother said to me. She was not speaking in anger.

I looked at my mother; that bitch was crazy. No wonder I smelled Stacey's damn oil when I was here. "Mama, I need for you to let me go before something bad happens. Please listen to me," I pleaded with her. "Stacey lied to you! You know that I would never do a thing like that. You know that I am not like you, for I do not go behind someone that I care about and do foul shit like that!" The volcano was going to erupt, and it was going to be bad for everyone. Once again, I felt so much hurt, pain and anger. Was this ever going to stop? Damn! I got cleansed to remove all this from me. I thought by taking that initiation that nothing else would be able to hurt me. I felt that the spirits had my back. I thought they would not allow these emotions to come back, but now they were here, hitting me in waves.

One of the church ladies released me and opened her bible. She began reading Psalm 23. I could feel the pain intensify as I knew that I would not be able to stop *Bella*.

"Come out of her, the Lord our God commands you to leave this body! You foul spirit of witchcraft!" the other lady screamed in my face. The other lady kept reciting *Psalm 23*

THE DESTRUCTION OF FAITH

repeatedly. I began to convulse, and I was shaking so severely that her grip loosened. I could not stop *Bella*, and I knew that she was going to take over.

"No, no, no," I muttered. I closed my eyes as I tried to fight *Bella* and shut out the noise that I was hearing. It felt like rushing water was filling my head, and I was not going to escape the flood that was approaching. I freed myself from that woman's hold as my body began to shake violently. I closed my eyes, and I started to see bursts of red light shooting past me. I could feel the heat from each light path as it flew past me, pulling pieces of my mind with it. I did not want to lose myself. I could hear rushing water in my ears, and I began to see tsunami-type waves move towards me. I wanted to scream as the waves moved closer, and one gigantic wave emerged on top of my head. I saw a woman riding this wave with long flowing hair and eyes were like fire. It was Bella. "NO!" I cried out internally.

Suddenly it went calm, and I opened my eyes. I blinked them several times, not believing what I was seeing. I saw Betty standing a few feet in front of me with blood running down what I could make of her face. It looked like she had been beaten severely in her face with a hard object. Betty was unrecognizable to me, but I knew who she was. She walked over to me and whispered in my ears. The wave crashed down upon me, and *Bella* took over.

177

CHAPTER 45
THEY KEEP LYING TO ME

THIS TIME I was aware of what was going on. I could see the fright on the two women's faces as she emerged. They looked at my mother, shook their heads, kissed their bibes, and started towards the front door. I guess their exorcism had not worked, and they were not ready to fight a losing battle.

"Please don't leave me here to face this demon on my own!" my mother cried.

"You better call Pastor. We ain't ready for this," one of the ladies said, running to the car. They both hurried inside the car and sped off.

Bella began laughing; it was more of a low growl as she started moving towards my mother. My mother was backing away from her, and whatever she was saying to her was making no sense. All I heard was water rushing in my ears. Stacey ran towards the front door to try to leave, but the door slammed in her face. *Bella* began forcing all the doors and windows closed. Stacey moved back towards Ruth stood beside her in disbelief. Neither of them could believe what they were experiencing. Stacey grabbed Ruth by the hand and led her to the couch. They both took a seat. They had to sit here and feel my pain now.

"Oh my God," Ruth whispered.

"It's going to be okay, Miss Ruth," Stacey said. "I can reach her."

Bella sat down, and all she could see was red. *Bella* heard something in her left ear. I could also listen to a voice telling me that I had to calm down and control my breathing. My ears no longer felt like they were filling with water, and I could hear more clearly. I began to listen to that voice speaking with me. I began to control my breathing as *Bella* tried to fight me to stay in control.

"Faith, please calm down," Stacey pleaded with me again. She was cowering like a small child beside Mama, and I could smell her fear.

"I do not care about how much money you got, bitch. I am going to get that demon out of you!" my mother screamed. Ruth began coming to her senses. She would not allow the devil to have power over her. She pushed Stacey away from her and stood up.

Bella had subsided for a little while, but I had no idea how long I could hold her back. *But what money?* I looked at my mother, and she appeared to have developed some confidence.

Ruth stood tall with her back erect. She had faced worse than this. "The devil is a lie, and he has no power over me. Do you think that I will allow a demon to come up in my house and take over? You got another thing coming!"

A guttural sound escaped me, and I laughed. "All my life, you have been abusing me, sleeping with my guys, and you even killed my baby. This right here is not what you want!"

When Betty appeared, she whispered in my ear that they both were lying. Betty told me how my mother had wanted Stacey to call her mom. She told me they attacked her. But my mother had given her the final blows which had killed her. I saw Betty still standing there, and she was smiling. These bitches had taken everything from me, and now they act like I am the one who needs to calm down? That I am the devil.

I could smell Kush, and I looked around. I smelled Freedom. Was he here too? I looked around the room, but I did not see him. I began to get this strong urge to leave, and *Bella* began to reside.

What the hell was going on?

I did not want Bella to go! I needed her to beat the shit them both, but something was preventing her from coming. I glanced over at Betty, and she had vanished. I needed her too. The water sounds were fading, and I had no idea what was going on. Bella had left too, and I did not want that; I wanted to destroy them for hurting me, but I could not. They were both staring at me with fear and hate on their faces. Slowly I got up from the chair and walked towards the front door. The doors flung open, and I walked out of the house.

CHAPTER 46
THE LIES CONTINUE

EVERYTHING THAT HAD JUST HAPPENED WAS unbelievable to me. I had never been able to control *Bella* before. I walked down the hill and headed in the direction of Poole Road. Something was pulling me to go to the bookstore. I had no idea what was leading me there. But I kept hearing that soft voice calling me, directing me and it was calming. All the rage that I had been feeling began to disappear, and I felt relaxed. I was feeling the way that I had felt last night after my initiation. I was no longer allowing my mind to focus on Mama and Stacey.

All the hurt that I was feeling was leaving me. It seemed the closer I got to the store, the calmer I was becoming. As I made my final steps to the store, I had completely calmed down. I walked into the store, and Nana was standing there with a bottle of clear liquid in her hands. It was as if she was waiting on me. "Go to the center and sit down," she instructed.

I walked thru the beaded doorway to the center and sat down. Yemi was there, and she removed my shoes. *What was going on?* Nana walked over to me, and she began pouring that clear liquid over my head. It smelled sweet and flora-like. I looked at the bottle, and it was Florida Water. She was telling me that it would calm me even more.

How did she know what I was experiencing? What did she do to me?

"I know that you have questions, but I need to tell you *Afua Fida* that you are connected to me now. Whatever you feel, I can feel it too, and I can control you."

Why did she call me by that name? My name was Faith. I did not like how that name sounded.

I tried to stand up because I was not too fond of the thought of her being able to sense me like that. I felt like she was invading me, but I felt like she needed to invade me; maybe this was what I needed to calm *Bella*. But still, something was not right, and I began to hate that I didn't heed Freedom's warning. I still had unfinished business to take care of with my mother and Stacey. Nana interrupted us.

"*Fuck that bitch*," I heard Bella say to me. "*She just wants to control us; she wants your power.*"

I shook my head, trying to escape her voice, but it would not be quiet. I thought Bella had left. She kept repeating the exact words over and over.

"Do not listen to that voice, do not listen to the *sunsum*. Your *kra* has been trying to protect you. But your *sunsum* is filled with so much pain that it has overpowered your *kra*. I am here to help you balance them out."

Nana Madou told me something that I had never heard of before, and I did not want to listen to any of it. "What are you talking about?" I asked her.

Yemi had gone and got me a glass of water. She was nervous, for her hand was shaking when she handed me the glass. I did not take it for her mother instructed her to place it on the floor. I smelled Kush again. I looked around for

THE DESTRUCTION OF FAITH

Freedom, but he was not there. I am tired of all these games. "Where is Freedom?" I asked them. "I can smell him."

"I am here." I heard his voice say, but I did not see him. Nana was now frowning, and she glanced over to the veil. I followed her eyes.

Was he behind the veil?

"Where are you?" I spoke.

"I am here with you," I heard him say.

"Where? I do not see you. Please help me," I sounded.

Nana moved to stand in front of me. She was trying to block my view from the veil. The tension came back into my head again. It sounded like he was speaking to me from behind the cover, and I was determined to see where he was. Every time I tried to see around Nana, she kept blocking me at every turn. *Bella* was demanding to take over, and I was trying to hold her back.

"Calm down, Faith," Freedom said to me.

"If you are behind that veil, come out now!" I shouted.

He did not reply to me, so I pushed Nana Madou aside and dashed for the veil. Yemi tried to grab me, but I managed to slip out of her grasp. I kept my eyes on the cover, not caring about them. As I made my way towards it, I could smell him strongly. His scent was coming from behind that white sheet. I jumped over a gray chair that was in my way, I was close to it, and as I lifted my hand to snatch it down, Nana Madou grabbed me!

"Freedom!" I screamed. There was a loud noise coming from the front of the bookstore. I could hear a woman's voice screaming and yelling. It was Mama!

CHAPTER 47
BELLA

I WAS STILL TRYING to move Nana Madou off of me when the doors flung open. It was my mother and Stacey. *How did they know where I was?*

"Get your hands off, my daughter!" I heard my mother shout. "Leave her alone! You got her all caught up in this voodoo shit!" My mother moved towards me, and she was trying to push Nana off of me. Nana Madou left me alone and stepped backward from us.

She fell against the chair, but she did not lose her footing. She stood straight up. "Faith is where she needs to be away from you," she spoke with calmness.

Does she always have to act like a fucking queen?

I stared at my mother, curious about how she was going to handle Nana. My mother comes off as being a bad bitch, but Nana stood tall and proud against her. Neither of them was willing to give each other their power. They both acted as they owned me.

I had fallen to the floor once Nana let me go. Stacey approached me. I had dropped to the floor once Nana let me go. Stacy was trying to help me stand. I glared at her. She

THE DESTRUCTION OF FAITH

must have seen something in my eyes, for she backed away from me.

"Leave her alone!" Yemi shouted, approaching us. She helped me stand.

"Bitch, who you are talking to!" Stacey shouted at her.

Yemi backed away from me. *I know she isn't afraid of Stacey.*

"That's right bitch, back the fuck up!" Stacey spat at her. That pissed me off. We are sisters now, and I will not let Stacey attack her like she did Betty. Before I could lash out at Stacey, we heard Nana's voice. She was speaking to my mother.

"Ruth, you need to sit down. It's your fault that Faith is like this." Nana motioned with her hand inviting her to take a seat.

"How the hell do you know my mother's name?" I said, focusing my attention back on her. I was going to deal with Stacey in a minute.

"I know many things about you," she replied, looking at me. She looked back to my mother. "You need to tell Faith the truth, and once you tell her the truth, she will be able to heal, and this will go away."

"Tell me the truth about what?" I was confused. *What was going on? What did she know that I did not know?*

"I do not understand what you're talking about," my mother retorted.

"I know what she is talking about," Stacey said.

Nana looked at Stacey. "Stacey is that why you came by here the other day. You got that potion from me to use on her mother?"

Stacey looked at me and then my mother.

"Wait a damn minute," spoke Mama. "What the hell is this lady talking about?" Mama directed that question towards Stacey.

Stacey began acting nervous. She found herself backed

against a wall. "Ruth, these people are crazy! I do not know what she is talking about!" Stacey was lying.

Then it dawned on me. I knew that I had seen a familiar car that day I was here, but I could not place the vehicle at that time. "Stacey, what is going on. " I said to her. I wanted to calm *Bella* down, but she would not allow it. No matter how powerful Nana Madou was, she was not stopping *Bella*. I could feel it.

"Tell her the truth," Yemi chided in. Once she heard her mother speak, she got her confidence back.

What did Yemi know?

Stacey began acting nervous, and I could sense that she would not handle her back against the wall. "Faith, your grandfather–" she started to say.

"It's not your place to tell her anything," Nana said, interrupting her.

"Tell me what?" I was confused and angry. "What about my grandfather? Are you trying to tell me?"

What did they know, and why was I being kept in the dark?

"Ruth, please tell your daughter the truth. Once you tell her the truth about who she is, this curse will go away from you. Your lie is the curse you placed on her life. You should have been telling her the truth," Nana said to my mother. She spoke to her with urgency. I needed to know what was going on.

My mother was now crying as she sat down in the chair with her face buried in her hands. Stacey was trying to speak, but she could not open her mouth. She was trying to say something, but she kept struggling to release the words. Nana must have done something to her mouth because it would not open. It was hilarious to me watching her clawing at her mouth.

My mother removed her face from her hands and stood up. I begin to feel sorry for her. I could not remember a time

THE DESTRUCTION OF FAITH

when I had seen her cry, and I wanted to embrace her. As I moved towards Mama, she regrouped. "I have nothing to tell that witch!"

A sharp pain raced through the back of my neck, and it felt like it hit the center of my brain. I winced in pain.

Nana shook her head, and she must have felt that pain when it hit the back of my neck because she fell on the floor. Yemi rushes to help her up. I could not stop the pain that I was feeling. I wanted to know what was going on. But to hear my mother call me a witch was to me like being called a bitch, and I wanted to hurt her.

Suddenly I heard Stacey shout out. "Your grandfather was your father!"

What did Stacey just say? Did you say that my grandfather was my father?

"How did you know that?" I heard Mama ask.

"I came here the other day to buy a potion from Nana Madou to get you to tell me the truth when I ask you certain questions. I used it on you when I bought you Chinese food home. It was to get you to tell me all your secrets. And you sang like a little bird trying to get out of her cage. You told me everything that *he* had done to you." Stacey declared. She was standing there shaking her head at my mother as if she had just told her off.

I am going to snap the head off that bitch!

My mother was crying, but she did not fold. She moved towards Stacey, and Stacey backed up. "You bitch! You have been using me this whole time and putting me against my daughter. I am going to kill you!"

Mama lunged for her, but Stacey darted out of the way, and mama fell on the floor. I moved to her to help her get up, but she pushed me away, "Get away from me, witch!" she cried. Mama got up from the floor slowly; she managed to take a seat using a gray chair to support her.

"Ma, is it true? Was grandaddy, is grandaddy my father? If it's true, I cannot believe this! You have lied to me! How could you keep this from me?" I exploded.

Stacey was laughing. I can't believe that this bitch was enjoying this. I swear when this is over, I'm going to kill her.

She was still laughing when she continued. "Your grandfather, I mean your father, used to rape your mother all the time. Soon it turned into an affair. Your mother was enjoying him fucking her, and she would let him fuck her anytime he felt like it."

"Close your damn mouth and do not say another word!" Mama screamed at her.

Stacey ignored her. "But then she got pregnant with you, and he no longer wanted her. He knew that you were his daughter, but he didn't want your grandmother to find out."

Mama stood up.

"Stacey, as I said, it's not your place to tell Faith. That is a family matter, and you need to stay out of it," Nana Madou said with sternness.

All I could do was look between Stacey and my mother. Mama was standing there looking disgusted, but I felt that she was a little relieved. Suddenly before I could stop myself, the tears began to fall as I stared at them. I started to feel a sharp pain in my chest. My heart was breaking.

I could not believe what I was hearing. My mother was a fucking whore, and she took all that shit out on me. "Is that why you beat me and abused me? I reminded you of him?" I said through my tears. "It explains why you always started trouble when we would go to visit him!"

Mama did not say a word, but Stacey continued. "But that's not half of it. Your mother killed your grandmother!"

What did she say? My mother is an evil person!

"Shut up bitch!" Mama shouted at Stacey. Ruth never wanted anyone to know that she had murdered her mother.

Stacey just kept going. "Yep, she knew that she had high blood pressure, so every day, she would call her and curse out, causing her to get stressed out. She caused your grandmother to have a stroke, and she died from that stroke. You did not know that did you? Your mother has been telling you lies your whole life."

I looked at Mama, and all the memories of all the hurt she had inflicted upon me began flooding my mind. All these years, I had to endure her wrath coming from a dark place inside of her. No wonder I was fucked up! All this time I could have been with my father! But then I began feeling anger towards him. He had raped my mother and even knew that I was his daughter. FUCK them both!!!! I could hear the waters coming back, and I did not want them to leave.

CHAPTER 48
EMERGENCE

MY HEAD WAS SPINNING, and I was erupting. I needed to sit down. I pulled a chair to me and sat down. Bella was whispering in my mind, and I no longer cared. I needed her! *Bella* took care of me, and she made sure that I was safe. *Bella* is my only friend, my true protector.

Mama had tried to attack Stacey again, and she ran from her. I could see her running towards the door. Yemi was one step ahead of her, jumping in front of Stacey; she blocked her from escaping. Whatever fear she had was gone. I glanced around the room, and I saw several of the women who had initiated enter the room and encircle Stacey so that she could not leave.

"Faith, tell them to move," Stacey begged. She was terrified and regretting what she had done.

I squinted. "These people are my family, and they got my back. Fuck you! You are not going anywhere." The tears had stopped. I could only feel *Bella*.

The pain in my head was fierce, and I was holding my head, screaming, trying to force the pain out, trying to stop

THE DESTRUCTION OF FAITH

the water from rushing in my head. I wish that she would come softly. Bella only knew my raw emotions of pain.

Please, Bell, you can take over but stop the pain!

"Faith, listen to the sound of my voice," I heard Nana say. She was interfering.

I was trying not to concentrate on her voice. The rushing water was too unbearable. I fell to my knees in pain and let out a loud shriek. *Bella* was laughing. She was ready.

"Faith," I heard Nana say again.

"Fuck that fake bitch!" Bella said to me.

"Fight her. Fight her!" Nana yelled at me.

I was trying, but I was too weak. I could not fight *Bella*. She was overpowering me. Maybe I had a mistake. Doesn't everyone need a second chance? I began to smell Kush, and I knew Freedom had to be here. He just had to be because he needed to protect me. Freedom had told me that he was here to protect me. That is what he told me. I looked around the room, and then I saw the veil begin to move. It was flapping as if a strong wind was making it move. Everyone was staring at the cover, trying to figure out what was going to happen. All I could smell was Freedom. His scent was intoxicating. I hide to fight to stay. Suddenly we all heard a ripping noise as the veil split.

The earthen pot began to shake as the pain in my head collided with the tremors of the vessel. "Please stop!" I screamed.

I managed to stand up again and what I saw made me froze. I saw hands coming from out of the pot. The whole room was quiet now as we watched it shake against whoever was coming out. I saw the shoulders rise above the rim of the vessel. A face appeared, and their eyes were closed. I blinked my eyes several times at what was happening before me. I saw Freedoms' face as he opened his eyes. Blue slime slid off him as he stepped out of the pot.

Oh my god, what was he?

The pain in my head erupted as I heard him call my name. It was excruciating, and as I tried to press my hands hard against my face, it did not help me. I looked around the room, hoping that someone would help me! Everyone was watching Freedom emerge from the earthen pot like a god. With each step he took, the slime was disappearing.

"Faith," Freedom said as he walked towards me.

"No-no-no," I muttered. I wanted him to stay away. He was a liar, just like everyone else in my life.

"Faith, please let me help you," Freedom begged.

I saw Nana Madou had run to Freedom and handed him some clothes. I glanced over at my sisters, who initiated with me, and they were on their knees with their head bows. I looked at Yemi as she went and stood by her mother. They both knelt to the floor.

I screamed as I fell to the floor. I was falling down that black hole screaming. There was nothing that I could do to stop *Bella*. *Bella* smiled at me as she began emerging.

ACKNOWLEDGMENTS

I want to acknowledge Barbara Hartzler for the beautiful ideas she offered me during this process.

I give thanks to my Ancestors for the beautiful experiences that I went through to share them with the world. I give thanks to my husband for his patience during my writing process. I give thanks to my family and friends for their support and encouraging words.

ABOUT THE AUTHOR

Queen Zoaya Counts was born in Stamford, Connecticut, in the year 1965. Her first published poem was titled *"The Fly."* She was only five years old. When she attended high school, she majored in Honors English, becoming interested in Creative Writing.

Queen Zoaya began journal writing which became collections of short stories. The first short story she wrote was titled, *Candy*. She is also the author of *The Dark Goddess, Ghetto Champagne, The Icy House, Onyx, and Shante's Place: A collection of Poems*.

In the early 2000's she became initiated into Santeria and Palo Mayombe. Several years after that, she received her rites of passage into Voodoo. She will introduce you to Spirits throughout her works, whom she loves, and hopefully, they will help you better understand your spiritual path.

www.zoayaworksllc.com

Twitter @LlcZoaya
Instagram @rahlioness
Tik Tok @rahlioness

Made in the USA
Monee, IL
07 October 2024